Situationz

by
D'Vine Pen

ISBN:

Situationz

Proudly self-published through Divine Legacy Publishing, www.divinelegacypublishing.com

Dedication

Chapter 1
JaNae

I grew up as an only child who longed for siblings. Thankfully one of my best friends, Denise, was the perfect substitution. Growing up, I remember her mother telling us about her sorority, Psi Kappa Psi. As a young girl, I couldn't fathom some of the details from her stories. Her experience alone made me look forward to college. All she talked about were the parties, pledging, and community service. Okay, okay, she had me at parties, but it was at that moment I realized that I wanted to be a part of something greater. With both Denise and my other bestie Brianna by my side, we made a pact to become Psi Kapps together. If Denise's mother taught us anything with her stories, it was joining a sorority creates a bond of sisterhood that can never be replaced, and the day is finally here.

Now, at age 21, I'm on top of the world. I'm finally crossing the burning sands of the illustrious sorority of Psi Kappa Psi, Incorporated. And I'm hella excited. As planned, Denise and Brianna are both by my side. No. More. Pledging. Thank God! I'm telling you, I couldn't take another night of that shit without losing my entire mind or going off on somebody's ass.

We started with seventeen girls on our pledge line and only twelve of us survived. We endured eight weeks of taking orders, being yelled at, taking wood, sleepless nights, and hiding from our big sisters whenever possible. I constantly asked, "Lord, when is it going to end?" At one point, my line sisters and I were going to the dorms where some of our big sisters' boyfriends lived because we had to wake them up with Starbucks and serenade them at 7:00 am sharp. It was either that or there would be hell to pay later that night. Not only was it time consuming, it was expensive as well.

The shortest person on our line, standing right under 5 feet tall is our ace, Shayna. She has pipes on her that can give the R&B Divas a run for their money. During those early morning jam sessions for the guys, we sang anything from Aaliyah's "At Your Best" to Bryson Tiller's "Don't". I can't sing a lick so I would help with the beat, snapping my fingers and doing the choreography that Bri made up for each routine while our other line sisters harmonized with Shayna. Trust me, I have no issues being the Michelle Williams of the group.

Our mixture of talents and creativity made it all come together like clockwork. Each morning we broke into two groups to get our tasks done faster since we all had to attend early morning classes. On certain days, we had to do routines dressed as our favorite old school groups like TLC, Boys II Men, even the damn Supreme's, and it went on for weeks until the guys begged our Big Sisters to stop making us wake them up. That was enough to drive anybody batshit crazy. Looking back at it, it was hilarious though. These are things that made us bond and get to know each other.

I am the deuce of the line, not too much taller than Shayna at 5 feet 3 inches. I'm short and thicka than a snicka, but ain't nothin' sweet about me. I was blessed with the line name Poetic Justice because of the way I would spit poems off the dome when we were on line. Our Dean, Traci, gave me an unusual topic to spit about one night while at a poetry set because she'd heard that my tongue is lethal and, if I say so myself, my pen game will bring you to tears if you cross me.

"Number 2," Traci yelled. "Get yo ass over here right now! I heard you think you Maya Angelou or some-thing, so let me hear what you gotta say about these fuck niggas around here," she yelled, sounding more pissed off than usual.

Her on-again, off-again boyfriend had just gotten caught up with his side chick, yet again. That idiot let social media get the best of him. The side chick posted pictures of them together and tagged him in the post. Before he could take the photos down, it was too late and Traci was pissed. His ass was straight busted. I knew it was my time to shine, so a few minutes later I hit her with this:

Made a mockery of my
feelings with a tongue gilded in
gold lies. Yet, to no surprise
A coward stood before me full
of mumble raps and lullabies.
All that was asked of you
was truth and honesty,
Plus…my love, to be your one

and only, obviously.
Too hard to follow this equation.
But so easy to dip in between
my sheets soaking wet in need of my ocean,
Quick to leave you leaking and paralyzed.
I fault myself for not looking
deeper past the mask you wear,
R.I.P to a Fuck Nigga Disguised!

After that, Poetic Justice was born. I solidified my name and was one step closer to being in the sisterhood of my dreams.

At other times, our line had moments where we'd laugh all night from the skits we created to perform for our Big Sisters. There were even times when we shared stories about which of our Big Sisters we wanted to slap first as soon as our pledging hell was over. But I can honestly say that going through this journey created bonds between the women on our line that will last for a lifetime because, at the end of the day, only the strong survived. Now we are more than friends who went through some rough shit together; we are sisters.

Now that it's over, I look back on everything we went through and realize its worth. Having my best friends during the madness made the experience that much better. I laugh to myself as I think about all of the stories I now have to tell my future grandkids. Being on line is an important thing of my past, and now I'm ready for the present, because tonight is our night! It's our official coming out show. If I must say so myself, my makeup is flawless and this curly 22 inch running down my back is a *way* better look than the ponytail and cap I've been rocking while on line. Not being able to get my hair and nails done was torture! Now, I'm back to my usual and definitely feeling myself!

No one on campus even knew Psi Kappa Psi had a line. The rumor mill was flying and everyone was trying to figure out who the newest members of the distinguished Psi Kapps were. There were strict instructions from the old heads not to tell a soul about our process. No one could know we had a line. Hell, that's what happened to number sixteen. Her cousin asked one of the prophytes to look out for her. She was kicked off the line the next day. The old heads played no games! Once sixteen was gone, the rest started falling like flies. Number thirteen couldn't take that wood and quit the first day we got it. Number four had a damn attitude problem and didn't like people in her face. I'm glad she kicked rocks because she kept us in trouble with that mouth of hers; she never knew when to shut up. Number ten didn't even give us a reason why she quit, she just never came back and stopped answering our calls. I thought that was weak as hell. And number nine couldn't afford the $850 initiation fee. No love lost, it just wasn't their time.

Our moment is finally here. Here we go! We are masked and ready to be revealed during out neophyte presentation. One after one we are lined up, dressed in black Psi Kappa Psi, Inc. shirts that are sliced all over, giving the crowd peek-a-boo action and exposing our purple bras like it's a Kanye West design. We are coming through classy and sexy. Our line names and numbers run across our backs, letting the world know which organization we represent. The black, high waist pants accent our curves and make it comfortable for us to move in. Black and gold embellished ankle boots complete our ensemble. It's time to let the show begin!

Stepping through the party as hard as we possibly can, our line, known as The Justice League, makes its way into the party. We are representing proudly with precision and passion in each step. We know our coming out show is the official announcement that Psi Kappa Psi is returning to the yard. We have to shake the Houston campus up and send everyone on a social media frenzy.

At the sound of three hand claps, my line sisters and I begin chanting, "I loooooove Psi Kappa Psi, yeah baby I love it. No other one above it! I love it! I love it! I love it!" The crowd roars and cheers, signaling that our arrival is like the birth of a new nation on campus.

As the audience continues to applaud, we do our best to make a statement with every step, clap, and movement. We shout, "Make room for twelve of the prettiest females on campus coming through…representing purple and gold because we're *all* so cold!"

We have sisters from all over the region here to celebrate and, since this is the first line our chapter has had in over five years, our goal is to come out strong and show out. The Alpha Gamma chapter of Psi Kappa Psi at the University of Houston was suspended because of acts of hazing that lead to lawsuits and pledges in the hospital due to alcohol poisoning. With the graduate chapter in place, and transfers from other schools working together, the national board had to petition the university to re-establish Psi Kappa Psi. There's a hands on graduate chapter present to oversee our prophytes and make sure it doesn't happen again. The women from our graduate chapter were pulled from nearby colleges and universities and understand the importance of a balanced pledge process. We understand they serve a purpose and work together for the greater good of revamping our chapter. It feels so good to say "our chapter".. And after gaining the trust of the university, Psi Kapp is back in action. I know our line will work hard to gain the respect we deserve and put Psi Kapp back on the map.

Hearing people in the crowd has me nervous as hell, but I know I'm shining and have to stay focused on my moves and line sisters.

"Get it Deuce!" I hear someone yell.

"I see you Nae!" shouts someone else.

There's no better hypeman than the audience and our prophytes presenting us on campus. This moment alone is for the nay-sayers and haters on campus, letting them know we're back and here to stay, bitches!

Once we hit the stage, my line sisters and I branch off and put on a mini step show. Our big sisters have no idea what we have planned for the night. My line sisters are not stopping and showing true discipline and it is driving the crowd wild! Cardi B's song "Bodak Yellow" roars through the speakers and all twelve of us are giving it all we have. We are literally leaving it all on the stage, showing all the other sororities on campus that they need to step their game up because we are *not* to be fucked with. While stepping, we use our entire bodies with a mixture of thunderous footsteps, slinging our hair from left to right, and dropping it low to show the sexiness of true females in charge. Twirling canes between our legs and doing stunts continue to drive the crowd wild. At the end, we throw the canes off of the stage and jump in front of the onlookers.

Running our index finger across our throats to signify it is over, we chant, "Move out the way! Step back. Psi Kappa Psi is back! Move out the way! Step back. Psi Kappa Psi is back!" I don't think the crowd anticipated a show like this from us. The standing ovation is proof the show was better than expected. I know our founders would be proud. We stand still as the crowd settles and one by one we are reintroduced to the University of Houston campus. We each begin to step up and throw our masks off, as if to say, "Recognize who stands before you!"

Looking into the crowd, I can see my mother and the rest of my family supporting me and my girls. My mom was worried about me joining any sorority. For her to see how everything turned out, I know it set her mind at ease. The introductions are over, now it's time to party.

Sorors shower us with gifts that range from one of a kind handmade crafts to t-shirts and of course our line jackets all night long. We worked damn hard for these. My mom is the greatest. She made me, Denise, and Brianna gift baskets that include personalized drinking glasses, key chains, car decals, and blankets. It's a sweet surprise.

"Mommy you really are the best. Thank you sooooo much," I say, kissing her all over her face.

"Okay, okay, okay, that's enough crazy child! You know I'll do anything for my girls. Now, don't let all of this distract you from your classes. If Denise's mom wouldn't have talked me into it, I wouldn't have been on board. I need you to graduate and make something of yourself young lady," she preaches.

"Yes ma'am."

"I have to work in the morning, so kiss your aunties and cousins so we can get out of here and let y'all get back to the party. I am proud of you baby."

"I love you Mommy, let me walk you out."

While walking my family to the guest parking lot, I run in to party-goers that continuously congratulate me. The friends I have from other sororities scold me for not giving them a heads up on my pledge process. They understand the secrecy because they were all in my shoes once. I can't lie; I live for the attention and acknowledgement.

One by one, I thank my family for coming out and supporting me. As they drive off, I'm left alone in the crisp night air with my own thoughts. It dawns on me that the worst part is over, and the best is yet to come. There were times that my line sisters and I had to talk each other off of the ledge and stop each other from quitting or fighting. Hell, the process made us so crazy at times, we almost turned against each other. I had to be the voice of reason to get us through this and re-mind everyone why we were here in the first place. Now, we can say we made it and it's time to finally act a fool, damn it!

Walking back in to the party, I see my girl Brianna giving people life on the dance floor. That girl has been dancing since she came out of the womb, and dance is truly her gift. She started posting her original dance routines on her YouTube channel about a year ago, and now she's an internet sensation. I'm pretty sure that had a lot to do with my sorority wanting her as a member. Can you say, "Step show prize money?"

I am in awe with everything at this point. The love and the support are real. I'm absolutely high on the attention.

"Excuse me Ma, I just wanted to say congrats," I hear a nice baritone voice say from behind me. Turning around, I notice he's not too bad on the eyes either.

"Why thank you stranger. And you are?" I'm single and he is fine, so yes I am flirting.

"My cousin invited me and my boys to the party. Said she wanted to show off her neos, and now I see why. You definitely did your thing, yo!"

At this point, I know I am blushing hard and his east coast swag is making Ms. Kitty tingle. Somebody needs to dust the cobwebs off this thing. I've been so focused on pledging and keeping my GPA up, that I haven't had time to think about a man. And Mr. East Coast has my eyes wide open right now.

"Well thank you. I'm trying to catch the accent. Where are you from?" I ask, looking him up and down. He looks so damn scrumptious. I'm loving the Yankee fitted cap and Timberland boots that he's wearing. It's a plus that he's not wearing those lame ass skinny jeans. I can tell his body is muscular and the t-shirt is hugging his arms just right. His lips have my mind on one thing only, wondering what that mouth do. It's on and pop-ping, because I am definitely going to have him.

"I'm from Jersey, and the name is James by the way. I just had to find out who you were because in that sea of purple, all I could see was you," he confesses through the most beautiful smile I've ever seen. My panties in-stantly become wet and, as if on cue, an oldie but goodie comes through the speakers and Adina How-ard starts belting out "T- shirt and my panties on…" The music has me swaying to the beat. Can you say clean up on aisle five?

"You have my undivided attention, Mr. East Coast. My name is JaNae."

Grabbing my hand, James leads me to the dance floor like he knows what I am thinking. Our bodies are getting acquainted with one another, slowly grinding to the beat. Two songs later we are in our own world. There is no need for words; our body language is speaking volumes as we stare into each other's eyes. Our chemistry is so strong that we have completely tuned everyone out and neither of us realizes that we are now being watched by half of the party. I'm definitely feeling his vibe. Damn!

It is time to get the party jumping again so the DJ breaks our sultry glare when he starts mixing in the beat for Juvenile's "Back That Azz Up". You know that always get the crowd going. Just as I muster up the courage to say something to James, Denise and Brianna drag me away so we can go stroll with our line sisters and prophytes. I glance back at him with the "I'm sorry" look on my face, and he assures me with a head nod that it is cool.

"Sorry girl, we didn't pledge to not step or stroll," Brianna says with her dance central ass.

"Bitch, don't think I didn't catch the full blown fuck fest y'all had going on out on the floor before we snatched that ass up," Denise says, laughing.

"I had to get 'em. He was talking all good and next thing I know, we body to body. That boy accent tho… He had me at Yo Ma…Ohhhhh," I tell my girls.

"Alright sis, I see you! I suggest you do something with it before these thirsty heifers get a whiff of him," Brianna says.

Denise and Brianna know I plan on doing just that.

We represent our sorority all night long. Song after song, we let everybody know we came to wreck shop on the yard. So they're either rolling with us or need to be prepared to get rolled over, cause honey it's a new day. By the time the lights come on at 2am, I have sweated all my curls out and everybody in the place knows our names. And Mr. East Coast is nowhere in sight. Oh well, catch you later baby.

Chapter 2
Brianna

Sitting in my sister's dance practice with her and the other girls is amazing. I've been watching them blossom over the last three months and seeing them come out of their shells is a wonderful sight. My sister, Daja, is a part of the city-wide cotillion hosted by the Bright Girl's Foundation that has dedicated many years of service to help young ladies develop social graces for a lifetime of success. It's a little too bourgeois for my taste because of the ballroom dancing and wedding dresses floating around. But, the scholarships they give make it worthwhile. Daja asked the coordinators if I could join the choreography team to bring something new to the event. Dancing and choreographing are right up my alley. Since my sister is truly my heartbeat, this is not a problem. Normally, I would have done it for free, but I'm not turning down a paycheck. I like earning extra money. Let's face it, I am the true definition of a broke ass college student. It's also nice that I am finally getting recognition from my YouTube channel.

I try to be a good role-model for my sister by giving

her opportunities that I didn't have. I had to make things happen for myself, and I don't want my baby sister to have to worry about that. For instance, I wanted to go to public school with my friends, but my mom and I made sure she went to private school by finding scholarships and work study programs. I danced at the recreational center, but we pay for her to have classes for tap, jazz, and hip-hop dancing at a prestige studio.

Our mother and father divorced when we were young, but our father is still a big part of our lives. My mother was determined not to change the lifestyle to which we were accustomed to by uprooting us from the home where we grew up. Our parents had a knock-down, drag out battle in court resulting in her keeping our home and getting child support and my father's visitation being set in stone. Even though things didn't work out with our momma, we were still his baby girls and he made sure that we knew that we were special. He never missed our important events, and he planned date nights for us so we knew we were important to him. Daddy wasn't like most men who abandon their children after divorce or separation. They both worked hard to make sure we had a nice life. I still like to help out as much as I can.

"Looking good ladies," I say to the girls. "I love all of the improvement. Let's take it from the top. 5, 6, 7, 8..."

The girls begin to do the dance moves I taught them, and they look great. I'm so proud of them. After practice is over, I give Daja a ride home. It is nice to spend some quality time with my baby sister.

"I'm surprised you want to ride with me Ms. Daja. Doesn't your boo, Marc, always take you home?" I ask.

"Of course, but he's hanging out with some of his boys today. I told him not to worry about it. That I could roll with you," she responds.

"Alright, you know I don't mind. Let's hit up Netti's Burger Stand since it's on the corner. I'm starving, and I'm ordering a double cheese bacon burger with mushrooms," I say, licking my lips just thinking about the delectable menu full of greasy junk foods.

Netti's is known for their famous chili cheese dogs, Philly cheese steaks, and juicy burgers. If you have a sweet tooth, they have just the right fix with their super thick malt or milkshakes, slushies, and strawberry dipped ice cream cones, just to name a few of the fan favorites. I only come every blue moon because I'll end up with sugar diabetes messing with these treats. As a kid, whenever daddy brought us to celebrate a special occasion, like a birthday or a good report card, the triple fudge brownie a la mode covered in sprinkles was my favorite dessert to order.

"Girl, where do you put it all?" Daja asks. "You're like a little garbage disposal."

After finding a parking space and walking up to order, Daja laughs and says, "I see they finally added a few healthy alternatives to that heart clogging menu so I'll take a Caesar salad and a sweet tea. Some of us can't be a forever-size-6 like you heifer."

"Girl, bye! I'll take them size D's and that ghetto booty any day. Ol' thick, cute self," I say playfully nudging her. This girl doesn't appreciate the bomb ass shape she has. I bet Marc, her high school love, does though.

"Sis, you're not trying to lose weight for Marc, are you?" I ask.

"Hell no, I'm not trying to lose weight. I'm just trying to be healthy. My man loves every curve on this body. Trust!" she says, smiling as if she is reminiscing on a secret only she and Marc knows.

I know she's beyond the birds and bees talk. I don't want to know if my little sister is getting hers, but what am I expecting? She is 17 years old, beautiful, and has a body that won't quit. Her boyfriend is a basketball phenomenon whose been getting scouted since his freshman year of high school. Thinking their hormones haven't taken over would be stupid.

"Daja, I know you and Marc are in love, but promise to protect yourself. Niggas these days aren't thinking about you or the consequences of their actions. All they want is a quick nut, and then it's on to the next. I've been there, trust me."

"Look Bri, I know you're trying to look out, but damn." She rolls her eyes and releases a hard sigh. "Not every man is gonna do me like Paul did you, Brianna. I get that he played you and left you high and dry while you were pregnant, but don't put your past situation in my lap. Me and my bae are good. He's going to the league and I'm going to medical school to be a doctor. So…we're straight." She tells me matter-of-factly.

Damn. She didn't have to bring up Paul and all that old shit. Just mentioning the situation is a stab in the heart. Paul is a distant memory I would rather keep buried in the past. I loved him. Or so my simple-minded ass thought at the time. We dated for less than a year, and our relationship was full of drama. Paul was two years older than me so, of course, I thought I was doing something big by dating an upper classman. There were always whispers of Paul and other girls. When confronted, lies rolled off of his tongue like a flowing faucet. He had an excuse for everything. And being young and naive, I allowed it to go on for the duration of our so-called relationship. I loved him though. And I wanted to keep him in my life. Like any teenaged boy, he was ready to make things physical between us and I knew I couldn't hold out on him any longer. With the way things were going, he was going to leave me. JaNae and Denise told me to dump his ass when the rumors started. But Paul had game for days, and he had my mind gone completely. Back then whatever he said was gold.

Against my better judgment, I gave in and lost my virginity to him thinking we were destined to be together. Once sex entered the picture, things got a little better between us. It was like he couldn't get enough. He had me sneaking out of the house and skipping school to be with him. Since my mother was working two jobs at the time, all I had to do was keep my grades up and my actions went unnoticed. Everything was good until it wasn't. When my period was late, I found out I was pregnant, and he left me. It was typical bullshit. He knew that he was the only person I had been with but said the baby wasn't his. The hardest thing I ever had to do was sit in front of my parents and tell them the devastating news.

My mom screamed until she was hoarse, and my father was heartbroken. He marched me right over to Paul's house with tears running down my face to have a conversation with him and his parents. That was a huge mistake. They had no sympathy and offered to help pay for an abortion, something I knew I couldn't do. Paul willingly signed over his parental rights and wanted nothing to do with me or our unborn child. Feeling like I had no support, and not wanting to cause my mother any further stress, I gave our daughter up for adoption. That time in my life was something like a *16 and Pregnant* episode but without the cameras. I miss my baby girl every day. I receive pictures from her adoptive parents, but still wonder and dream about the daughter I named Ashley Renee.

Daja had brought up a harsh reality that I am still not ready to face. Before I can think about it, my open palm contacts her face and I slapped that attitude right out of her ass. She knew she was wrong when she said it, and her eyes begin to well up with tears. She has the nerve to try to raise her hand at me, but I give her a look that tells her death is coming for her for even thinking about it.

She looks around at the other patrons waiting for their food and storms off to the car as I scream, "Fuck it then, you think you grown so do you! Let's go!"

Thank God the food was ready. I grab the to go containers as soon as they call my name, barely saying, "Thanks," as Daja paces back and forth by the car. I don't unlock the door for her right away; her walking around should cool her off a bit. Once I make it to the car, we both jump in and she slams my car door shut, and then I pull off to take her ass home. I have other shit that I can be doing. There's a Psi Kapp meeting coming up and I need to talk to JaNae and Denise about it before we go.

"Bitch, I'm tellin' momma," she sobs.

"Tell her and see if she'll slap your silly ass too!" I yell back. "I'll call her for you!"

I pick up the phone and call mom, handing Daja the phone after the first ring.

Chapter 3
Denise

Shit is getting real. I am preparing for the nursing program to become a registered nurse specializing in pediatric care. Now that I am really getting in to my core classes, they are kicking my ass. I've always loved children and medicine, and I am not going to let anything distract me. The threat of my parents cutting me off may have something to do with it as well. As long as I'm in school with a GPA of 3.0 or better, my parents will fund everything. My mom is a total control freak and is up my ass on a weekly basis about my grades. At the end of the semester she wants them in her hand. Growing up, I was always told that the money spent on my private school education was an investment and I shouldn't take it lightly. In her eyes, my degree is a return on their investment.

I took a smaller work load this semester so I could pledge Psi Kapp with JaNae and Brianna. If it wasn't my mother's sorority, she might have gone nuts. It made me a legacy, since I followed in her footsteps. Fooled me for thinking I'd be given an automatic pass.

The selection portion was no issue, but they pledged my ass just as hard as any of my other line sisters for eight long weeks. Saying, "thank you Jesus! It is over!" is an understatement. No more Big Sister this or Big Sister that. No more bullshit. Now, I can't lie, some of it was fun and brought my line together. Especially when we did things like stay up all night studying our sorority's history and going on scavenger hunts all over campus. We shed plenty of tears because those hoes were throwing wood on us, but we learned to work as a team and it made us tighter in the end. One thing we learned is that wood is a motivator. No one took more than two pieces before bumping each other out of the way. They are literally my ride-or-die bitches.

Things with bae have been going pretty good. Al is so sweet and attentive, when he has the time to spend with me. I would love to see him more, but I know he is busy with school and his fraternity. I don't want to be *that chick* so, for now, I'm going to play it cool. Speak of the devil, look who's on my FaceTime.

"Hey gorgeous, you trying to see ya boy tonight? I'm on some chill stuff, and I wanted to hang out with my baby," he says.

Cheesing from ear to ear I say, "You know I do. Pick up some wings, and I know you got that green so let's blow one," I excitedly tell him.

"That's a bet babe. Unlock the door," Al slickly says before hanging up the phone.

I am glad he's stopping for food. It gives me time to get my place in order. I do a double check after cleaning up the crib to make sure everything looks perfect. My candles are on fleek and it smells good in here. I still have time to jump in the shower.

While I strip out of my sweaty clothes I take a look in the full-length mirror, tie up my faux locs, and give my body a once over. I'm starting to notice the definition in my arms and thighs. Possibly an outline of a six pack as well. That's what the fuck I am talking about! My trainer, Cherri, is definitely worth every penny.

Jumping in the shower, I give this pretty pussy of mine a quick shave and wash up. I quickly put on lotion and some sexy lingerie and head to my bedroom to wait. Laying alone and ready in bed, my desires to be touched can only be fulfilled by my man. Now that I have crossed, it's time to come out of hiding with this relationship. I understood the secrecy while I was pledging. After all, my boo belongs to our brother fraternity and there were serious warnings about dating one of them while on line. It was a no-no. On top of that, I've heard plenty of warnings about them being the playboys who run our campus, but by then I'd already met Al and I wasn't about to let him go.

I secretly laughed my ass off when our old heads told us that they were off limits. Telling me that I am forbidden to do something is more like telling me to go full speed ahead. Aside from that, look at him. Swag and sexiness oozes from his pores. Standing at six feet one inch tall, Al's muscular body is high yellow, and his pretty boy looks make him extremely fuckable. This brother has a style no one on campus can mess with. Those pink, juicy, irresistible lips, along with his light brown eyes put me in a trance that keeps me weak and coming back for more. He keeps a fresh cut, and he doesn't follow trends; he makes them. Truthfully, when we first met, I couldn't resist his picture-perfect smile and those dimples that are to die for and then some.

The first time Al caught my eye was at a welcome

back picnic thrown by the Greeks on campus. I loved my newfound freedom and independence of being away from my mother's watchful eye. My girls and I were freshman at the time, and JaNae's mission was for us to be as sociable as possible. We wanted to be known on campus and get on Psi Kappa Psi's radar. As the party got going, the DJ had the crowd moving and all of the students were having a good time. Fraternities and sororities started party hopping throughout the picnic to show off their skills and new strolls.

Looking across the park, I saw something I liked and he was gettin' it! I peeped him from a distance, so I could go unnoticed. There was no way anyone could miss this fine specimen of a man making his way through with his frat brothers. They were grinding, making sure to put emphasis on their signature moves, thrusting against some young ladies then smacking them on the butt when they were finished. Some of the females chosen for their little male bravado were offended, but I wasn't. I was *sooo* aroused, and silently wishing I was one of them. He eventually made his way over to our area with his brothers and they introduced themselves to the freshmen on campus.

As the semester went on, I ran into Al occasionally at various functions around campus. I would flirt and drop subtle clues in hopes that he would get the hint and get this love connection started. Surprisingly, it took a little longer than expected. He finally saw that I was throwing him mad flavor and asked me out. On a chilly winter night, I accompanied Al to the Houston Fall Festival. We both were looking forward to a night away from the collegiate life. Festivals always have a fun vibe with rides, games, and food. I knew I could find a turkey leg and a funnel cake with my name on them.

Al had no problem beating me at basketball or assisting me while we played an all-in-one mini golf game. He placed his hands on the putter while standing behind me, and whispered in my ear the whole time he was supposed to be helping me. Our cold night was starting to heat up. It was actually nice to get to know each other better. While we were on the Ferris Wheel looking out onto the beautiful downtown skyline, we laughed and talked about the way we grew up. It gave me a view into his background. It was then I realized that he was more than just a pretty face.

We enjoyed each other's company. Conversations between us flowed easily, and he kept a smile on my face. I remember thinking people are wrong about frat boys. After spending time with Al, I decided they couldn't all be the same, right? I've learned that the majority of fellas are hoes because of the stories I've heard from females around the dorms. But, none of those characteristics were displayed that night with Al, or any subsequent night. He was a complete gentleman, and my hands didn't touch a door while we were on our date.

Chivalry is definitely not dead. To my surprise, he catered to my every need and that night left me on my doorstep with a lingering kiss, wanting to do more. I accepted his embrace, welcoming his soft tongue and his lips pressed against mine. Lust began escaping my pours quickly due to lack of the *D*. Honestly, it had been awhile because I chose to put relationships on the back burner to keep my head on straight for school. I was determined to have a high GPA and, since I was known to lose focus when dating, I had to stay away. So, as temperatures started to rise, and hands started to roam, I knew it was time to call it a night. It was a hot and tempting goodbye kiss. Pushing the brakes was hard, but I couldn't go out like that on the first night. The hoe in me wanted to continue immediately, but I had to stick to my guns! Al said he respected my decision, and that date led to more, which is why he is mine now. In the end, I won. I learned how to separate school from relationships, and I got the man.

Now I'm sitting here, stroking this pretty kitty because it is in need of skin-to-skin contact. It's been longing for more than the 20 or 30-minute quickies I had to sneak around to get while pledging. My Big Sisters would have killed me if I got caught with Al, but he was worth the risk. I hear him come in, and then he's in the bed with me. Finally.

Al pinches and sucks my left nipple, and there is a fire starting to ignite from deep within. Al knows that's my shit and it drives me crazy. Tonight, there will be no rushing and we're making up for lost time. I'm so glad he finally made it and the wait is over. A low moan escapes my lips. Sensually switching between both breast so neither feels left out, Al makes sure they have his full attention. He starts to leave a trail of kisses from my C cups down to my cookie jar to put his money where his mouth is, literally.

As I watch him lick his way down Ms. Kitty opens up as if he's the only one with the password to unlock the hidden treasure. Toying with me, he kisses my thighs then watches me squirm with anticipation for what is to come. In my head, I scream, "JUST DO IT AL-READY!" This is my favorite part of sex, and I have a lot of pent up frustration that needs to be released. As if he reads my mind, he smiles, licks his lips, and then proceeds to give me head. The coolness of the air and warmth of his tongue is an amazing mixture to get my juices flowing.

His tongue play makes me shiver and bite my bottom lip. It's obviously been way to long. One thing I can say about my baby, he can eat a mean ass pussy and he knows it. Now, he's making his tongue swirl around my clit while he slides a finger inside me and plays her like his own personal instrument. This kind of penetration, while receiving oral, is the only way it should be done. The more I try to scoot away, the more intense it is until he locks my thighs down with his arms and goes to town on me, his face fully buried and engulfed in my wetness.

Lick for lick and pound for pound, I am in ecstasy as I moan louder and louder. I try to be quiet, but find myself thinking, *Fuck these neighbors 'cause at this point, they all know his name.* This boy is performing like a muthafuckin' champ! I can't breathe, and I feel like my head is about to pop off.

It's hard for me to handle when I feel like I'm about to explode and he tells me through glistening lips, "I'm not ready for you to cum yet. I want you cum on this dick for me."

He kisses me passionately, and I can taste my sweetness as he slowly enters into his kingdom. Working his way in, he looks deeply into my eyes. I love to watch him in his element. He moves in and out as he hits my walls in a circular motion. I can feel the outline of his six-pack flexing as he grinds on top of me in a missionary position. I promise ain't nothing holy going on in this bedroom.

Al is blessed and definitely packing. His thrusts go in deep, and his girth fills every inch of me. What more could a girl ask for in a man? The way his eyes lock on mine feel like he's looking in to my soul. It's too much, so I have to look away. Intimate moments like this let me know I'm sprung. It's uncontrollable. He's fully aware that the way he pleases me keeps me coming back.

"Oh my God, I can tell you missed me baby! Keep hittin' my spot!" I say.

The sound of the headboard hitting the wall is music to my ears. In this moment, with each stroke, I fall more and more in love with this man. Wrapping my legs around his muscular back, I'm getting my favorite muscle of all.

"Yeeeeeesss!" I scream in ecstasy.

"Baby, you can't go neglecting daddy like that no more. Leaving me out here all that time without feeling this. You got a nigga fucked up. Tell daddy you won't do it no more," he says while stroking even harder so I'd get the point.

"Daddy I won't…ooooh shit! I won't do it anymore," It's all I can say while he is beatin' it up, punishing me for neglecting him while I was on line. It. Feels. So. Good. Hell, what else can I do, but surrender?

"I'm going to show you why you won't," he says with a crooked smile on his face, while flipping me over to doggy style position. It's time for momma to put on a show, so I start throwing my ass back and bucking like there ain't no tomorrow.

I catch a glimpse of him in the mirror while he's hitting it from the back. My brown eyes lock with his intense gaze. It makes me arch my back and throw this ass back even more. When he starts smacking my ass, I know he's feeling this shit. It makes me grind extra hard. The sting from his palm makes me extremely wet.

I love how we fit together. Finding someone you're sexually compatible with isn't easy. You can go out and fuck anybody, but this shit right here is on a whole different level. Just like he is pulling my long hair, I want to pull him inside of me and tuck him in a place he's not able to leave.

"I want to try something babe, you down?" he asks me. Hell, I'm so caught in the moment that I don't care.

"Okay baby," I manage to say. Al slowly starts working one finger in and out of my ass to give me pleasure in another erogenous zone. I'm not feeling this at all, but I trust my man. I decide to relax and give it a chance since he asked nicely. I don't do ass games. Until Al came along, obviously. Plenty of my girlfriends told me that anal sex was good once you get past the initial discomfort of it all. It's hard to explain. Being caught up in the moment and feeling sexually liberated with Al has me ready to test any and every boundary with him. Hell, if he wants to get 50 Shades up in here, I would consider it. I always feel comfortable and wanted with him.

I now see in the past I've dealt with selfish men in their form of lovemaking. Let's be real, that was just young fucking. That's a huge issue with most guys, they don't take the time to please their partner or explore what makes them happy.

My natural juices flow from our sexual encounter, leaving a coat of clear liquid on the thin condom that separates us. Al checks on me repeatedly to make sure I'm okay. He keeps telling me to breath, knowing the overflow feeling of pleasure and pain is getting to me. I start rubbing my clit to get in the groove, and all I can say is that I'm in heaven. With the excitement of a new hole and the slow motion of his strokes, Al can't contain his excitement anymore. He begins to slightly pick up his pace while grunting, a sound I know oh so well. My baby is about to bust one, and I am heading to ecstasy with him.

"I'm about to cum baby," I yell at the top of my lungs while clutching the sheets. My body tenses up upon release. As I am cumming, all you can hear is the sloppy, dripping sound from my wetness as he thrusts in and out of his personal heaven. The sound of our moans mixing together reminds me of a beautiful melody.

"Ya boy did that! Got you climbin' the walls girl! Who love this big ol thang? Haaaa!" Al is really feeling himself. He doesn't have too long to gloat though. I have to catch my breath, and then I have something for that ass. I get out of his grip, take that magnum off of him, and inhale his dick. Both hands are twisting as my warm mouth moves up and down. Trust me when I say he ain't ready for this slurping action and he *definitely* isn't ready for me to get some ice out of my cup to set it off. He has no idea I'm skilled at giving head. The shock on his face makes me want to pull out all my tricks.

See, you have to display your superb head to a nigga bit-by-bit. Otherwise they won't know how to handle it. You can't give it to them all at once and since he was pulling tricks out the bag, I figure it's time to put it all on the table. Spitting on the dick and deep throating it past my usual consumption has his toes curling. He is getting off by the choking noises I make while he fills my mouth and touches the back of my throat. He has me stepping outside of my comfort zone, and I love it.

He tries to hide the pleasure he is feeling, but I look

in his face and it makes me go even harder as I think to myself, *Boo I have nothing but time so consider yourself my prey.* Working my magic, I decide not to leave his balls out of the party. While stroking him up and down, I take each one of them in my mouth to give them a little special attention. Al's thighs lock up and a vein begins to pop out of his forehead. Ding. Ding. Ding. I have officially found his special spot. I laugh at the fact that he can't handle this. Hearing him moan nonstop only fuels my fire to continue this fantastic fellatio! Al grips the back of my head and moves me to the rhythm of the slurping noise that fills the room.

His moans finally turn to the inevitable comment as he says, "Girl, what the fuck are you doing to me? No bitch…ever…did…ahhh!!" Now, that's how you celebrate. It is a wrap!

After a few moments of cuddling and catching our breath, Al falls asleep. It's what happens when you put that thang on your man. Deciding to let him rest, I head to the bathroom and get in the shower. The water feels good against my skin as I reminisce about the incredible sex we just had. I get so caught up in my thoughts, letting the water run down my back, I don't notice Al until he pulls the shower curtain wide open and presses his lips against mine, filling my lungs with smoke. I inhale the shotgun and enjoy the mellow feeling. Al, still fully naked, joins me in the shower.

"Can you hand me the soap please? I want to bathe you. Just relax and let your man take care of everything," he says.

"Thank you baby, I appreciate that."

It's just what a girl wants: her sexy ass man pampering her. Kissing me on the back of my neck while standing behind me, Al places my hands on the wall of the shower in front of me. After squeezing lavender and coconut oil over my body, he uses the loofah sponge gently on my skin and to caress my breasts. He uses his free hand to softly caress my nipples in a circular motion until they become erect. His gentle touch makes me tingle all over.

I turn to face him, and it feels like he is looking past my eyes and into my soul. At this very moment, he has me. I try to kiss him but he isn't having it and turns me around. He places my hands above my head on the wall again, whispering in my ear not to move as he brings his hands down all over my body. His touch, his breath on my neck, and the warmth of the water is driving me crazy. I feel his hardness press against me while his fingers find my treasure and begin to work their magic. Soft moans escape my mouth. Not being able to touch him is torture. Being disobedient, I reach out and touch his sides, moving closer to his manhood which is now fully erect. I stroke his penis and guide him in. Al aggressively pins my hands up yet again. This time he pins both wrists with one hand. Damn… I can't catch a break.

"You don't listen, so I'm going to have to teach you a lesson. I know you want this dick," he says, slowly sliding into me inch by inch. "Now I'm going to give it to you, so take it!" He pins me to the wall and thrusts into me hard and fast. All I can do is scream from ecstasy.

"I know you like it because this pussy gripping tighter and tighter." He is being a boss in my shit and he finally decides to release my hands.

"Turn around and spread that ass so daddy can get

in deeper," he whispers in my ear. Al put my left leg up on the ledge of the tub so he can hit it from a different angle. Why the hell did he go and do that for?

"Fuck baby… shit… you hittin… shiiiiit… you hittin my spot!" I yell.

Slapping my ass, he keeps a tight grip around my hips while slamming into me. I feel my knees starting to get weak. After several more thrusts, this negro turns me around. He gets down on both knees, pins me against the wall, throws my legs over his shoulders and starts to lick Ms. Kitty, making me scream because this shit is amazing.

"Baby, I can't get enough of tasting you," he manages to say between slurps. Nothing is sexier than a man at work, and you best believe Al is on his job. He doesn't have to worry about me going anywhere, that's for damn sure. My legs are tightening and my breathing is uncontrollable. Al stands up and pins me against the wall again as he slides back inside me. Now face-to-face with my lover, I wrap my legs around him. His thrusts become faster and faster, and I can't hold back this orgasm any longer. I began to moan in pleasure as Al starts to grunt from his release.

I collapse, leaning all of my body weight on him. We take turns washing each other off from head to toe. His touch is so electric yet soothing. My skin glistens in the afterglow against his body. Being shorter than him, my head falls right on his chest comfortably. Al runs his fingers through my damp hair as I gaze up at his cutie-pie smile. Wrapping his arms around my body, he bends down to kiss me passionately. I love the fact that he's affectionate. Most guys don't take the time to show you that you mean a damn thing to them. This is the era of

Netflix and Chill, and I'm not having it. I want and deserve more. After rinsing the soap off of each other's bodies, we climb out of the steamy shower.

"Let's go eat," he says.

"Didn't you get enough?" I ask playfully.

He grins and looks me up and down. "You ain't ready for another round." He laughs and walks out of the bathroom while I continue to dry off.

Still on the high from today's sex-a-thon, I'm not ready to come down. I walk out the bathroom and Al is sitting on the couch wrapped in his towel, hitting a blunt. Watching the smoke roll out of his mouth is intoxicating as I walk over and straddle him. He takes another hit, and I slowly press my lips against his as I inhale. I only need a few hits off the blunt and I'm good. All I can do is smile and be goofy snuggled under my bae.

"I'm glad that I'm done pledging so we don't have to be a secret anymore. I want to walk through the student union on the arm of my man," I say looking up at him seductively as I stand up to go to the kitchen to warm up the chicken he brought.

"Boo, you know I'm not into all that PDA stuff. You my girl, you know you my girl, so that's all that counts. You think I'm letting this good-good get away?" he asks. He looks me up and down from head to toe and licks those sexy ass lips.

"Babe, I don't see the problem with it. But okay," I say. I notice something lighting up out of the corner of my eye and realize it's his phone. It's vibrating like crazy. He has eight missed calls and six text messages.

"Someone is trying to reach you," I say.

"It's cool. I'm chilling with you. No one else matters."

His phone is on lock like a bitch, and I can't help but wonder what the fuck is going on here.

Chapter 4
Al

It's hard being *that nigga*, but somebody has to do it. Just tell these chicks what they want to hear, and they will sell their dreams for you. They make it so easy because all they do is talk. I don't have to ask for shit. One of my females keeps me laced. As soon as she receives that refund check, I get my cut and she takes me shopping. That's my Amber. Money is no object to her and if she wants to cash a nigga out, who am I to stop her? I met Amber during my freshman orientation while she was signing people into their dorms and giving them their orientation packages. She did the whole welcome speech, and then she touched my arm and said if I needed "anything at all" to let her know. She winked one of her pretty blue eyes at me and she's been down ever since. My dad shook his head at me. Amber has no drama; she's so chill and she is definitely my escape.

Then there's Ms. Rhonda, my high school sweetheart. We came to U of H together and if I knew then what I know now, I would've left her ass at home. It was like bringing sand to the beach. I'm glad she didn't see Amber slip me her number because I definitely had plans on hitting that from day one. Don't get me wrong, I care for Rhonda, but her being here is cramping my style. I did talk her into coming, it's only right I play my role. I don't want to lose her; I damn sure wasn't going to let another muthafucka dig my girl out. But, I'm not trying to be tied down either. The good thing is that she isn't into the collegiate experience, so I don't have to worry about her seeing me with one of my other girls. The bad thing is that she is getting real clingy, especially since I joined the frat. She gets pissed every time she does happen to run into me on campus because females stay in my grill. I just put my arm around her and walk away real cool. For every question she spits off, I have an answer like an automatic rifle. She always asks the same questions.

"Who are those girls?" she asks.

"Some girls from my sister sorority," I answer.

"Why didn't you introduce me?"

"Didn't know it was that serious," I tell her.

"I think if they are your friends, they should be my friends. It's like you're in a whole new world, and you're leaving me behind. You know I don't have time for all of that pledging stuff because I'm in the teaching program on an academic scholarship," she always says.

I don't have any plans on introducing her ass to anybody. To everybody else I'm out here and single, and that's how it is going to stay.

The newest one on my roster is the ever-so-sexy Denise. I hate to say it, but I'm addicted to her and her ass is a little too close to home for comfort. I got at her right before she joined my sister sorority. Had I known she was pledging, I wouldn't have fucked with her, and now it is too late. This one gives me everything I need sexually, and she is bad as fuck. I met her at our annual welcome back picnic while I was party hopping around the halo for a stroll off. Our eyes connected, and that shit knocked me off balance a little bit. My brother stepping behind me had to push me to snap me back into it. She was well put together, not over the top. She never acted like she was trying too hard.

Her caramel skin looked like it was kissed by the sun. She reminded me of my celebrity crush, Meagan Good. Her braids were pinned up, so you could see her face and those big, beautiful eyes of hers. Her lips stood out, painted a shiny hot pink, and when she licked them my dick jumped. The sundress she was wearing showed me perky titties and a round ass. All I saw was a body full of curves, and I had plans to ride every one of them. I've never chased a female before, but I had to find out who she was.

As the picnic went on, I kept my eye on her. I always saw her hanging out with her girls but never saw any of my brothers in her face, so I knew she wasn't a groupie. The more I paid attention to her, the more attracted I became. It was just something about her that had me instantly drawn to her. I had to break the ice right then. Funny thing was this chick actually had me nervous.

"Hey ladies, are you having a good time? Do you need anything?" I asked them with my eyes on the prize.

"I would like a drink if you don't mind and these are my girls, Nae and Bri," she said introducing them.

"And your name?" I asked.

"Denise," she said confidently.

"It's true what they say, beautiful women do run in

packs," I said spittin' at them hard.

"Okay playa, I see you," Nae said as all of the other cuties smiled. Playing it cool, I didn't push up on her immediately. I wanted to find out more information on her, to see if she was worth it. After knowing her for a few months, I wished I would've met her first. The juggling act is starting to get out of hand. I have to enjoy it while I can though. Damn, she walked into my life at the wrong time. I already had too much going on.

Chapter 5
JaNae

Wow, it is our first meeting since crossing, and now the Big Sisters are our equals. When we were on line, they felt like our enemies. I came to the meeting prepared and on time. I don't want to miss a minute. The student union conference room starts to fill up as members begin to come in one by one. So much love fills the room, reminding me of the reasons I joined a sorority: for the sisterhood and community service. It's good to see my line sisters. I love them, but after eight weeks of pledging and seeing them day in and day out, it was also nice to have a little break. Once everyone is present and accounted for, the meeting begins.

"First of all, ladies I would like to welcome all of our neos to their first business meeting. I know pledging was hard, but now the real work begins," Stacy, the president of our chapter states.

"Welcome ladies," comes from smiling faces all over the room. They were evil as hell while we were on line. It'll take some time to get used to their hugs and smiling faces. We were handed the agenda when we first walked in the conference room and Denise, Brianna, and I are impressed by their professionalism and flow of the meeting.

We start our meeting with a prayer and recite the pledge, then we discuss the chapter's old business before moving forward to new tasks. Finally, the floor is open to suggestions for our community service projects and fundraiser events. I don't know if anyone else is thinking it, but the suggestions from the old heads are old and tired. How can we come back on campus with a bang by selling church chocolates or going door-to-door to collect donations? The group text with my line sisters starts to go off.

> *Bri*: They can't be serious!
>
> *De-nice*: Do I really look like I'm going to beg anybody for money?
>
> *Denise*: I thought this sorority used to be the livest one on campus.
>
> *Shayna*: Snore fest! Wake me up when this is over. *Tamara*: Waste of time! I could be studying for a test!
>
> *Me*: Come on guys, let's hear everybody out. Ya'll speak up and make suggestions if you don't like what's being said. I feel you though, they really need to step it up.
>
> *Sean*: Nae, why you always gotta be so diplomatic? Forever the momma…LOL!!!
>
> *Bri*: LMAO
>
> *Kelly*: Momma Nae always saving hoes.
>
> *Denise*: The real question is why Stacy didn't take that damn weave out a year ago she had that Brazilian hair a Brazilian years bi-

hhhhh…

At this point, I burst out laughing and my girls are low key rolling. Everyone instantly turns around to look in my direction. Damn! Here goes my big mouth getting me in trouble, again. While giving my line sisters and I the evil eye, Stacy informs us of fines for cell phone usage during a meeting and asks if we have anything to add.

"Yes. During our process, my line sisters and I came up with ideas like hosting a speed dating event, having a poetry night, and a few parties off campus to pull in higher revenues. We also have several community service ideas to get our name recognized by the city and bring positive attention towards the sorority…" Kelly tries to say more before she is rudely cut off by Candice.

"Per the bylaws, that has to be run through the proper channels and voted on, so the answer is no! I am the grad chapter alum and this sorority will not be run like some 'girls gone wild' reality show. I don't need some Kim Kardashian wannabes as the face of the shield that I stand for!" Candice yells. I guess the bitter bitch decided to let us have a piece of her mind! One thing is for sure, she has me fucked up.

"First of all, Kelly you're not on line anymore so you do not have to address us as your Big Sisters," says Stacy. She rolls her eyes at Candice's rude ass and says, "Candice does have somewhat of a point, as harsh as it may sound. There is a protocol in place, which you will learn in time."

Come to find out, Candice was one of the graduate members that nationals asked to help bring our chapter back to the campus. Obviously older than us, she's been a member of the organization for 6 years. Yet that shit was not very sisterly. She was also a past president. I see what time it is now, so I discreetly hit the group chat again.

Me: Meet me at my house when we get out.

My whole line agrees to meet up by nodding their heads in my direction. I can tell by the looks on their faces that we all have a problem.

About 20 minutes later, the meeting is adjourned. Stacey and Candice are in deep conversation across the room and for the life of me I can't figure out what they are saying. Candice looks in our direction and storms off. I don't know who pissed in her Cheerios this morning, but Stacy is shaking her head as Candice walks in our direction to leave the room.

"Hey neos, I'm sorry for the way Candice was acting in the meeting. There is a much nicer way for her to get her point across. All you have to do is create a proposal and submit it to me. As the president, if I approve the proposal, the chapter as a whole has to vote on it. Remember, this is not a dictatorship, and everyone has a voice," Stacy says before she gives each of us a hug and heads out.

My line sisters and I walk about 15 minutes across campus to my dorm in Parks Tower. I have two cool roommates, and I'm blessed. I have heard crazy horror stories of the wrong people being paired together ending in fights, racial tension, and theft. I am lucky to have never had that problem. Though I wish I could be with Brianna and Denise, scholarship restrictions and paperwork deadlines prevented us from living together since we are all in different programs. I'm happy to avoid all of that drama because I need peace where I lay my head.

Once we get settled in, we decide to break into groups of threes and each group has to come up with a proposal for one fundraiser and one community service activity that will fuck their heads up. We have more than enough connections between the 12 of us to get it done. We all share the sentiment that it is a new day!

"Y'all hungry?" I ask. I can't stand inviting people over and not offering something to eat or drink. I am a southern belle to the heart.

"Anybody want to order pizza?" Kelly asks as she begins to look online for promos.

"I'm actually in the mood to cook a 'lil something for y'all. How about Cajun?" I ask.

"Girl, you know I'm down! I love your Cajun food," Brianna adds, with her greedy ass. Lord only knows where she puts it all.

Cooking is one of my escapes from the day- to-day hustle and bustle. Next to writing, it's my favorite thing to do. I love to see the look on someone's face when the flavors begin to dance on their tongue. Getting compliments on a meal I have prepared or a poem puts me on a natural high, and I can never get enough.

A few of the girls have to leave so I'll have to catch up with them another time. I head to the kitchen and begin to chop bell peppers and onions. Denise comes in the kitchen with a devilish grin.

"Best friend, whatever happened to the cutie you were dancing with at the party?" she asks.

A smile instantly creeps upon my face as I begin thinking about him, Mr. East Coast. The cutie with the perfect lips.

"All I know is that his name is James and he is from

New Jersey. I haven't seen him since that night. No number. No nothing," I say as I reminisce about that night at the party.

"He sure would be a nice distraction. Y'all looked so cute together, and you had chemistry like y'all have known each other for years," Brianna adds, sneaking up from behind and listening to the conversation.

"You saw it too? Even though I was only with him for a short period of time, it felt so much longer. Hey, like I always say, if it's meant to be, it will be." I try to sound nonchalant, but I'm secretly wishing he'd asked someone for my number and called me. "Once I finish sautéing the shrimp, the jambalaya will be ready. Let's get the drinks poured and fix these plates so we can eat. The bread is in the oven and is almost ready too."

The aroma of Cajun spices light the room up and has everyone's mouths watering. Shrimp and sausage jambalaya with salad and garlic bread is an easy yet impressive meal to prepare. My besties and line sisters pitch in to help set the table and get the salad ready so we can hurry up and eat. I can tell they are more than hungry by the expeditious way they are fixing these plates and drinks. That's what dorm life does to you when you don't get home cooked meals on the regular. We sit around the living room on the couch and the floor, bless our food, and dig in to eat. It is nice to have this productive down time with my girls. As we drink wine and fill our bellies, my thoughts drift back to James.

Chapter 6
Brianna

My African Ensemble class is my favorite class this semester. The combination of the movements and beat of the drum helps me escape. When I dance, I feel so free. I am in my own zone and nobody can touch me. The instructor, Lana, is everything! She wears Liberian garb proudly to pay homage to her family's homeland. She keeps up with all forms of dancing from ballet and hip hop, to line and tribal dances. I can honestly say that Lana is more than an instructor. We have formed a friendship over dance.

"Lana, I appreciate you letting me use your dance space when you're not instructing girl," I say thankfully.

"Bri, it's never a problem. Anytime I can help another sister who has as much passion for dance as I do, it's my pleasure."

"Since you said that, I was hoping that you would work on something with me. You know I post videos of my performances, so I want to choreograph something we can do together. I have the Beyoncé and Shakira "Beautiful Lie" concept in mind. We can mirror each other back and forth," I say as I cross my fingers in my mind. I know this routine will be epic.

"Sounds like fun! It's about time we do a collaboration anyway. I need to get my following up. Plus, you know anything I can do to help my girl, I will," Lana says as she reaches out to give me an assuring hug, which I truly appreciate. I don't have many friends outside of JaNae and Denise and a few of my line sisters. The friends I do have, I cherish.

Bouncing ideas off of someone else's head who knows where I'm coming from makes working on concepts for the video exhilarating. We start working on choreography and, before we know it, three hours pass. When you're doing what you love, time is no object. Now, it's time for me to get my sweaty ass out of here and head home for my Friday night television shows. I'm going to stop by the student union and get a bite to eat before I hit my dorm room.

I decide to be a good girl and get a grilled chicken wrap instead of the usual burger or pizza they offer. Smiling from ear to ear about my day, I don't even notice who is standing in front of me. Chase Reynolds! My long-standing, grade school crush! What is he doing here? I look like a hot sweaty mess. How can this be happening? Locking eyes, he looks at me and smiles.

"Bri, is that you? What's going on girl?!" he asks. His smile automatically displays those heartbreaking dimples. He pulls me into a hug, and I have no choice but to enter his space. Why does he have this effect on me?

"Nothing much this way. Excuse the way I look, I just got out of the dance studio," I state shyly as I run my fingers through my damp bob haircut.

"You were always modest and cute by the way. It's

really good running into you, it's long overdue. I don't see anything wrong with the way you look."

"Forever smooth Chase. What are you doing here? I thought you went off to college somewhere else," I asked curiously, knowing damn well that I know exactly where he went.

"I did… I had a full ride to several universities, but the freedom was too much to handle. The parties, the women, and the drugs got me kicked off the team," he admits, looking slightly embarrassed.

"Oh. I had no idea, and I hate all of that happened. I'm not sorry it brought you back home, though." It's crazy how I grew some balls to flirt with this grown ass man that I have had a crush on since middle school.

"Bri, I wouldn't mind catching up with you further, but I'm pretty sure you've got to get back to your man and everything," he inquires on the low, waiting on an answer. He thinks he slick.

"If there's anyone waiting on me, I can be persuaded to make them wait. If you want to meet me in the lounge in my dorm, I wouldn't mind carrying on this conversation. Give me a few minutes to get myself together, and I'll meet you in the P Hall lounge."

"That's a bet. I'll be over there in, let's say, an hour," Chase says. I watch him walk out the door and secretly screaming on the inside. Damn, even his walk attracts attention and women are looking at him non-stop as he walks through the union area.

I grab my food and get the heck out of dodge. The sun is setting, and the weather is warm which makes me crave that shower even more. Walking two buildings over to the newest unisex dormitories on campus, I reach Phillips Hall which we call P Hall. It was named after Samuel Phillips, an alumni who donated millions of dollars toward campus preservation. In a daze over running into Chase, I immediately head to my room to get my shower caddy and towels. While showering, I wash my slender frame from head to toe using *A Thousand Wishes,* one of my favorite scents from Bath and Body Works. It's guaranteed to turn heads with the festive blend of sparkling champagne, crystal peonies, and almond cream. I layer my scents with the lotion and body spray for the perfect combination of sweetness that cannot be ignored.

Once I'm finished with my daily bathroom ritual, I head to my room in a hurry because I am a stickler for time. I hate it when people are late, so I try to be punctual. I'm seriously nervous and excited to see him. Getting my shit together, I blow dry my hair, throw a few curls in it, and finger comb it. While looking for something cute to throw on, I decide on my favorite burgundy mid-drift top from Pink by Victoria Secret's that slightly shows my stomach and a pair of black tights. My outfit is complete with comfortable pair of black and white slides. Before I hit the door, I put on a little shear shimmer lip gloss so my lips will be popping.

With a few minutes to spare, I'm headed to the lounge. I take the elevator down three floors and the closer I get to our designated meeting spot, the more butterflies start to flutter in my stomach. As the elevator signals that I have made it to the lobby, I exit and head to the very busy lounge. It includes pool tables, high definition televisions, and several gaming systems that can be checked out. The amenities offered are one of the reasons the dorm is so expensive.

Taking the two steps down into the sunken area, I see Chase with two other guys that live in P Hall. They are all engulfed in the basketball game displayed on the large screen HD television. Once he notices me, a smile creeps across his lips. He daps his boys up and walks toward me to embrace me in yet another hug.

"Damn you smell good, and you got all extra cute for ya boy," Chase says, laughing and raising up my hand to spin me around giving me a once over.

"Yo ass is so silly. I'm not gone play with you. So come on, let's sit down and catch up." I say, leading him over to the sofa in a more secluded area of the huge lounge. I turn on the TV, which is already tuned in to VH1. *Brown Sugar,* an oldie-but- goodie movie starring Taye Diggs and Sanaa Lathan, is on so I don't change the channel. I'm a sucker for black romance movies. Getting comfortable on the plush sofa, Chase pulls me close to him. I have no desire to resist so I oblige him.

The conversation between us is so natural and the smile never leaves my face. Reminiscing with Chase about high school and catching up on our friends and families is just what I need. Surprisingly, he confesses that he had a thing for me in high school, but I was with Paul and I had absolutely no idea. Maybe I was just too blind to see it.

As dusk turns to dawn, and light begins to peek its way across the window pane, I can't believe that we have been up watching movies and talking all night.

"Bri, I had a good time just sitting here talking to you. No pressure, no bullshit. You have no idea how much I appreciate that with everything that's been going on since I came back home," Chase says. He looks at me so sweetly while brushing my hair behind my ear with his finger. He comes closer, leaning in and capturing my lips with his. I can taste a hint of Carmex as our lips lock. Even though I am surprised, his actions are welcomed.

Chase pulls me on to his lap and holds me close. I have absolutely no escape, and I like it. This scene really isn't my style, but I'm living in the moment. For once, I'm thinking about my own needs. I guess I'm feeling this shit a little too hard because I start to moan and forget where I am. Now that I'm lost in the sauce, it's time to regain a little control.

As much as I don't want to, I pull back.

"I'm sorry. I don't even know if you have a dude, and I'm just kissing all on you. My bad," he states politely as he helps me to my feet and off of his lap.

"Well if we choose to have another conversation, I will let you know. Since you have my number now, you can call me. Now, let me get a few hours of sleep before I head to practice with these girls for Cotillion. It's only a few weeks away, and I need to make sure they are on point. My name is on the line."

"Okay *Americas Next Best Dance Crew*!" he says as we both laughed uncontrollably.

"Boy, go head!" I reach up to give him a quick peck so I can leave, but he engulfs me in another breathtaking kiss. Damn it feels so good. When he releases me, I bite my lip a little, showing that I don't want this to end.

"Alright, I know you need to get some rest. It's just that I've wanted to do that for a long time. Oh and trust, we are going to continue this conversation. But for now, I'm out!"

With that being said, he walks away. I stand there and for the second time watch him walk away. I can see him in the distance as I watch him through the tall windows. Slowly but surely, he is out of sight. Bringing my hand up to my lips, they creep into a soft smile. What have I just gotten myself into?

Chapter 7
JaNae

Being the overachiever that I am, I got us the green light to do poetry night as a fundraiser for the sorority. With the presentation that we put on, it was a no brainer: put on a show, give the people what they want, and make money. The sorority needs the exposure. The bottom line is that we can conduct business and have a good time as well. The plans include guest poets that are already established in the area with a good following, a live DJ, and sexy waitresses who can work the crowd.

I was meeting up with the crew for some much-needed girl time and to do some check-ins for the event. What better place to catch up than the nail salon? My nails and toes stay beautiful all year round. Believe me, you won't catch me slipping with chipped polish. Me and my girls have been going to Exxclusive Nail Bar for the last four years, and nothing about that is going to change any time soon. Lisa is my nail tech and that woman has the hands of an angel. By the time she gets done rubbing my feet and a possible three to four glasses of wine later, whatever silly problems that might have been bothering me when I walk in are out the door when I leave.

"Will Miss Brianna and Miss Denise be joining you today?" Lisa asks as she pours my first glass of wine. Before I can answer, they both walk through the door.

"Heeeeey sis, I missed you," Denise says as she sash-ays into the room. "Lisa, I see you over there pouring up. Add two more glasses boo," she says, a new Louis Vuitton bag in hand. This heifer must have had a good day because she is glowing.

"What's up Sorors?" I greet them both with a kiss on the cheek.

"Girl today is a real spa day. I just cashed my first big YouTube check from my channel reaching over 100,000 followers and over a million views on the last video I posted with me and Lana doing a new dance number we put together. Spa day on me y'all!!!!!" Brianna crazy ass dancing around making it rain. Lisa brings over our glasses and we celebrate with our girl. We are so proud of her. Real friends want to see each other win, and we have that.

"Denise, have you had any luck in securing a spot for poetry night? I'm ready to wrap up this event," I say.

Pulling out her rose gold iPhone, Ms. Thing makes a few clicks and rattles off, "The Red Tail Café is an un-derground jazz club and they usually offer open mic on Tuesdays, but we're bringing in the college crowd on Thursday for our event. The club gives you a chill, laid back vibe. It's for everybody. There's no dress code, so all are welcome. We've got the venue from 6-11pm since the event is from 7-10 pm. We get the money from the door and they get the bar and kitchen sales. I suggest we have our own waiter staff, which is cool for our girls to make a little money that night on their own. We will have menu options, as well as a signature drink of choice. Depending on how this event goes, we can get a contract for a set night monthly or weekly."

"Sis, you did that! I have Sean and Kelly in charge of décor. I want it fly, but not over the top. Tamara and Bri are over PR, flyers, advertisements, and blowing up social media for the event. Things are really coming together. Now we just need the poets," I say as I check things off of my to-do list.

"Excuse me *Poetic Justice*. I know you're going to bless the mic," Brianna says.

"I don't know. I didn't have the idea to showcase myself. I just want artists to have somewhere to go to express themselves freely. We don't have enough exposure. Plus ya'll know I want to throw it in Candice's face that we can throw a successful event and represent the right way."

"I feel you, that bitch was so out of line.

"Don't worry, we've got this," Brianna assures me.

"Now that we got business out of the way, who's got tea ya'll? Spill it!" I say, ready to hear about some juicy sexcapades. Especially since I haven't had any of my own. All I have is my faithful Jack Rabbit vibrator keeping me warm at night, and I swear that shit is getting old.

"You will never believe who I ran into," Brianna says as she stands up to wash her hands during her manicure.

"Bitch who? You're blushing hard as hell," Denise

questions as she high-fives me.

"Do you happen to remember Chase Reynolds?"

"Chase Reynolds…from high school?" I ask.

"*The* Chase Reynolds your ass has been crushing on since birth?" Denise adds.

"I thought he took his fine ass out of state for college somewhere?" I say.

"Yep, that Chase. He did go away for school, but he is back now. I ran into him in the student union and long story short, we talked all night. I really don't know what to think about it," Brianna confesses.

"Ya'll talked all night huh? Bullshit! Just talking doesn't make you walk around on cloud nine like that. Did you finally get a piece? Somebody needs to dust the cobwebs off that thang," I chime in while we all crack up.

"Very funny. But after we talked, we just kissed. It all happened so fast that I couldn't do anything but enjoy it. Being in his arms sent electricity through my body and took my breath away. It's a feeling I've never felt before, so it was somewhat scary. By the way, I get the D when needed. You're the one that needs to slow your busy ass down and get broke off before you explode. Those batteries can only work for so long," Brianna says. These heifers are dying, literally hollering from laughing so hard.

"I'm sorry sis, you know that shit was funny," Denise tries to console me, but all I can do is laugh.

If you can't beat 'em, join 'em. The crazy thing is that I have a funny way of putting everything before my love life, so they are right.

"Al is doing way more than kissing… I can't get

enough. We were at the mall doing a little shopping. That's where I picked up this Louie bag. My daddy said that was all I was getting for my birthday so don't ask for shit else! On our way to the food court Al pulled me into the family bathroom and locked the door. He pulled them panties to the side, ripped that foil pack off that condom, and went to work. Head down ass up! He gave me that 20 minute pounding like it was nothing. When we walked out of the bathroom, this woman just shook her head at us, so I winked at her. You better take your offended ass on somewhere, hell! Just thinking about his …ohhhhhhhhhhh," Denise said now fanning herself.

"Damn, I need to get on your level. Get it biiiiiihhhh!" I say, high fiving her crazy ass. That poor old lady.

Everybody's love life is going well, except for mine. I guess my turn will come one day. Guys stare at me all the time, but don't ask me out. Do men not know how to date anymore? How is it easy to ask me for a piece of ass, but not give me a chance to get to know you? I want to know how these niggas grew up. Who raised them? Find out where their people are from. Is that too much to ask? I digress.

Before we head back to our oh-so-busy schedules, we insist that Brianna let us leave Lisa and her girls a tip since she paid for our services. We thank Lisa and set up our next appointment before heading out. Walking out of the nail shop and feeling good off that Moscato, my best friends and I go our separate ways. It's moments like this that I cherish the most. However, that warm and fuzzy feeling doesn't last long. Denise calls me in a panic and yelling. During the time we were getting pampered, her tires had been slashed. Who would have the nerve to do some shit like that?

Chapter 8
Denise

Sitting with my Dad at Discount Tires was not what I had planned to do with my day. I'm still baffled. Why would someone do this, and who would want to do this to me? Hell, I don't bother anybody.

"Your mother is not pleased with this 'ghetto mess,' as she calls it," my father informs me.

"But Daaaaddy, Momma is overreacting as usual. This time I actually didn't do anything. Is she ever going to stop riding me, dang?!" I said pouting. I get up and walk away dramatically, all teary-eyed because I know daddy can't stand to see his baby girl cry.

"Denise, I agree with her so that's all that's going to be said about that. You have to take more responsibility for yourself. We are paying hand over foot for you to go to college and have an apartment, so you can focus on school. We expect more from you." I know not to protest when Daddy puts his foot down.

"Let's go grab a bite to eat until this car is finished girl, with your spoiled self. Lord what will your future husband do with you?" Daddy says, shaking his head.

At least he's smiling.

"Thanks Daddy. Just what I need, a little father and daughter time. It's not every day that I get you all to myself," I say, batting my eyes and hoping my dad will take me to my favorite restaurant. I'm starving.

"I know I've been extremely busy with the law firm, but sweetie I'm always here for you. I'm actually looking to slow things down a lot more so your mother and I can do some overdue traveling. Working hard all of these years is nothing if you don't take time to enjoy it," my dad tells me.

He is absolutely *the* greatest man on this earth. How he puts up with my mom, I don't know. I swear she stays on ten, but to each his own. I know I am biased because I am my daddy's baby girl. My brother, on the other hand, is close to my mom.

"Come on Niecy let's catch the shuttle to Pappadeaux's to have some lunch and hang out. You also need to tell me about this boy you're seeing." I love it when he calls me Niecy. That's his special nickname for me.

"Daddy it's no big deal yet. We're just dating. I want to see how it goes before I bring him around."

"Little girl, these little wanna be thugs just want what's between your legs. That is your treasure, and it shouldn't be taken lightly. Don't be out here treating these knuckleheads like your husband if they are not. You'll catch that one later in life, and you'll see why I say that. Hell, I use to be one. Your daddy had females lined up and a man can smell the weakness a mile away. They use it as control, so make sure you protect yourself mentally and physically," my daddy says, giving me a stern talking to but he put me down with the game. That's why I respect him so much.

"I hear you daddy. Like I SAID, it's just the beginning and I'm getting to know him myself. If he is worthy of bringing home, you will be the first to meet him. I know he's not ready for the third degree from mom. She's going to go in!"

"You know how your momma is, so he better be careful," he said.

I love spending quality time with my dad, even if it is for a crazy reason. Hey, I'll take it. Pulling up to the home of my favorite Cajun food, my mouth starts to water as I breathe in all the Cajun spices. We sit at the packed bar and my dad orders a Corona while I order a glass of Moscato. We chit chat about the game that's on, enjoying each other's company. Twenty minutes after placing our order, the waitress places grilled tilapia over dirty rice in front of me and a crawfish platter in front of him. This is what I call southern living.

Over lunch my dad and I talked about everything from my classes to politics. He is the type of person who knows a little bit about everything. I have no idea what his law firm is going to do without him when he retires.

"Daddy, thank you so much for stopping your busy schedule to come help me out."

"Niecy, you know it's never a problem. You know I'm a phone call away baby," my dad tells me as he hugs me and kisses me on the cheek. He can put a smile my face when nobody else can. Getting off the shuttle, I walk over to my Civic. I am glad that this ordeal is over. All of a sudden, I feel weak and my head starts spinning. I try to catch my breath as I lean against my car. After what seemed like forever, I was finally getting back to normal. What the fuck is going on with me? One thing that being in the nursing program has taught me is that you don't ignore your body. Even though it's probably nothing, I will be making an appointment first thing in the morning.

Chapter 9
Brianna

The time has come to showcase my girls to the world at the cotillion. Our last practice was successful, ending yesterday at noon. The girls have been dancing their hearts out for me and as far as I am concerned they are ready. There is no need to push them any further. All they need to be worried about is getting dressed up and beautiful.

I haven't really spoken with Daja since our blow up. Even though I am pissed with her, I miss my baby sister. Sisters fight. I'll be the bigger person and holler at her about it later. For now, I need to get dressed and head to the venue.

I pull up to the Belforte Ballroom. These people are really putting on a show. Fancy cars and bougie black folks are everywhere. They live for this mess. This cotillion is the coming out party for the *who's who* of the upper echelon in the black community. Many sponsors and business owners are here, including the mayor and all of the parents pushing their kids to so-called greatness. Hey, if they like it, I love it. I am all for the scholarships, but the rest of this song and dance they can keep. I was a bit too much of a rebel or a free spirit in my day. I wouldn't have made it.

I walk into the ballroom, and I'm in awe of the beautiful décor and the wall to wall elegance. I walk back out to the grand lobby to take in the décor. The theme is *A Night in Paris*. Exquisite chandeliers and centerpieces with candles and crystals grace the ballroom. It is very simple, yet romantic. The tables also have name tags for all of the attendees. At my assigned table, I see my name, my mother and father, and we are alongside Denise and JaNae. All are prepared to pour out love and support for both Daja and myself, which means a lot.

I head to the back to check on my little ladies and see Marc, Daja's boyfriend, in the corner shaking hands and smiling with a few well-known businessmen. The people around here take sports very seriously, and I can bet money that they are trying to get the scoop on where he's going to college before the official announcement. I smile and wave at him, then keep it moving. Lord, my sister has a mess on her hands with that little cutie.

I enter the dressing area to see one beauty after another. Every single one of them took it to another level. This is no longer the usual down south cotillion; they are dressed in everything from Vera Wang to Carolina Herrera and anything else fresh out of Vogue. This is one of the reasons each young lady needs to find a sponsor three years in advance to help cover expenses. My damn wedding probably won't cost as much as one of these dresses, but to see the looks on their faces is priceless.

I approach Daja while she's putting the finishing touches on her hair. Tears well my eyes as I look at my baby sister in the mirror. Me and momma are both proud of her. I have to admit she's no longer a baby, though. She's an amazing young woman.

"Babe, I just wanted to come and tell you good luck tonight. My God, you look stunning. I seriously hardly recognized you," I gush trying not to let the tears fall.

"Bri, I have to say I'm so sorry for the way I spoke to you. I was wrong, and you didn't deserve that. I'm stressed the hell out. SAT's are coming up, this cotillion, and keeping my grades up…I'm so overwhelmed," Daja speaks as tears run down her cheeks.

"Enough of all that! Tonight, all you have to worry about is being beautiful, something you got naturally because you look just like me honey. We're going to deal with the rest later. We're sisters so we're going to fight and make up until the end of time. Now, you've got a fine man waiting to escort you in front of all these bougie ass people. Let's do what we came to do. Let me fix this make-up so we can get to this."

We both laugh and talk as we count down to the start time. This year's coordinator comes in to let us know we have a few minutes until go time and leads us all in prayer.

"Father God, please guide our steps in today's event and let these children continue to show dignity and grace as they are presented to the city as the brilliantly talented and beautiful young ladies they are. In Jesus name we pray, Amen."

"Amen," we say in unison around the room accompanied by applause.

"Ladies, I am proud of each and every one of you for all of your hard work and dedication. When I asked you to stay for an extra hour or come in early, you all complained but came back. You put your social lives on hold and gave me your all. For that, I am grateful. Now get out there and make me look good," I tell them before I head out to take my seat after blowing them kisses.

I make my way across the now crowded room, and my family and friends are already seated. As I exchange hugs and kisses with everyone, I can feel the excitement as the events begin. One by one, each couple is announced, along with the scholarships they received and the colleges or universities they plan to attend. There're a total of twenty-five couples who take their place on the floor. They perform an elegant synchronized dance that is just beautiful. Everyone is on point and doesn't miss a beat. The young men are leading the ladies with strength and poise. Each one of the girls glide across the floor as if they had been doing the dance all their lives.

Once the performance is complete, many thanks are given to the sponsors and parents. R&B sensation H.E.R does an intimate performance. She sings the roof off of the place. Jessica Care Moore, a spoken word artist from Detroit, controls the crowd as she speaks about how black lives matter. She could have been no more than a ten with such powerful words.

We finally make it to the moment I have been waiting on all night. No more wedding dresses or stuffy tuxedos. The kids have changed into fly urban clothing. Coming in from every direction, they begin to swarm the room. There's chaos everywhere. The surprise routine is now set in motion. Dancing in my seat, I am doing the routine with them. You can see the look of shock across the room, then enjoyment. Everyone is out of their shells and enjoying life. Certain participants who were included in the routine are pulled out of the crowd. Kids are dancing on tables; it's amazing. Everyone is having a wonderful time, which was my vision. I wanted the event to be something fun to attend, not a bore. To my surprise the kids pull me up, Daja being the ring leader, for me to finish up the ending. I am in rare form as I take the stage over. I feel like Debbie Allen from *FAME* or something. Dance is life!

When the music stops, we receive a standing ovation. "This was put together by Brianna Wright everyone. She deserves credit for her brilliant creativity; and to these young people, absolutely excellent job!" Ms. Cynthia says over the microphone. She has been the head chair over the cotillion for the last 15 years. She claps along with the rest of the room. Feeling a sense of pride, I just bow and say thank you. An elephant sized weight has now been lifted from my shoulders. My parents shower me with hugs and kisses. When I chose dance as my major they didn't understand my incredible love for the art. Seeing the pride in their faces, I can see that they finally get it. I'm thankful for the kids because, without them, my vision wouldn't have come to be.

All at once, those who formed around me split like the Red Sea forming a line on each side of me. I don't even notice due to the high that I'm coming off from the show. Slowly walking towards me is a tall drink of water. Handsome, smooth as can be, and smiling, and showing those chocolate dimples. Chase comes my way holding the most beautiful bouquet of assorted flowers I have ever seen. Covering my mouth, I look toward JaNae and Denise because this has their names written all over it.

"Well, we had to make sure your night was perfect sis. We asked Chase to be your escort for the night,"

JaNae says.

"I see he showed up and showed out!" Denise's crazy ass adds.

Standing in front of me, Chase hands me a large bouquet and gently kisses me on the lips for the world to see. Then, the applause get even louder.

"I'm so proud of you baby," Chase whispers in my ear. "Oh yes I'm doing this!"

Hell, I feel like I just won Ms. America or something.

Chapter 10
JaNae

I have to go check on my girl Denise. She has been acting strange pretty much since the cotillion. I had to drag her ass out of bed for her to even go, and that wasn't like her at all. I'm going to straight pop up on that ass. I have to lay eyes on her. I haven't seen her on campus, and she didn't come to our last sorority meeting. Nobody else saw an issue with it, but I know better. As I approach her building, I see a girl walking up to my home girl's car mumbling to herself. I ride by slow and watch the girl in my rear-view mirror. What the fuck was she doing? Next thing I know, she burns off. I park and then go back to check things out. It looks like her crazy ass left a note on her car that says:

Welcome to the family bitch. Hope you like playing babysitter. You fucking with the wrong one.

With the letter was a sonogram. Oh hell naw! Al's pretty ass is a hoe. Better yet, he was a hoe-ass- nigga for doing my girl like this. The name on the sonogram was blacked out, so I don't even know who the mother is. Man, why did I have to walk up on this Maury shit? That's what I get for trying to do a good deed. I need to find me some damn business ASAP!

I walk up to the front door and knock then put my ear to the door. I don't hear anything, so I knock a few more times. Still nothing. Obviously she is here because her car is outside. I'm glad I have a spare key. Carefully moving through the townhome, I don't see anything out of place. I head upstairs to find Denise in bed with her Beats on her ears and zoned out. No wonder she didn't hear the door.

"Excuse me ma'am, where the hell have you been?" I say, waving my hand in her face, startling the hell out of her. My friend looks like she's been through hell and back.

"Girl, what are you doing here? I'm not in the best of moods." As soon as Denise says that, she springs out of bed covering her mouth on the way to the toilet. I follow her to the bathroom to check on her.

"If you are sick that's all you had to…" I enter the bathroom and stop dead in my tracks at what looks like 7 or 8 pregnancy tests. Reading them, I see the word pregnant, or two lines, or plus signs. Damn! No wonder she went into hiding. After washing her face and brushing her teeth, my friend just looks at me and cries. So I cry with her.

"Nae, what am I going to do? How will I even finish school? I haven't been able to move too far from the toilet as it is. I'm either throwing up or sleep," Denise sobs.

"Have you told Al yet? What did he say?" I ask. "He had the nerve to be happy. Yet, I haven't

seen him. I don't even know what to say to my momma and daddy. You know how my momma is. My parents already warned me that if I mess up they are cutting me off. Fuck!"

"You know we're all here for you. I promise your momma and daddy will get over it," I say, trying to console her. Now definitely isn't the time to tell her about the crazy chick and the note. Shit just got real! I *am* going to get to the bottom of this mess though; that is for damn sure. I know exactly where to find Al's slimy ass. At some point he will be in the union or the frat house. This nigga has two females pregnant at the same damn time. This is some real- life *Love and Hip Hop* type shit. If I didn't see it with my own eyes, I wouldn't believe it.

Chapter 11
Denise

Currently, I'm sitting in the home I grew up in, where I pretty much was denied nothing, listening to my mother yell at me.

"You can't be opening your legs to every pissy tailed negro running around here. I don't tell you this shit for my health. I'm trying to raise you to have a future, not to be somebody's damn baby momma out here on welfare. What more do I have to do? Harold you better get your daughter!" As annoying as my mom is, she's right. I know now what needs to be done.

"Niecy, do you know what you want to do? This is your decision, not ours. Either way you will be fine. People have babies every day," my father reassures me. He always has my back, and Lord knows I appreciate it. His words are full of comfort, but his eyes show that I let him down.

"Daddy, I'm sure I'm not going to keep it," I say, crying my eyes out. I knew better than what I was doing, yet I still got caught up. Wrapped in my daddy's arms, I tell him I'm sorry repeatedly. I'm surprised when my mother joins our embrace.

"Baby it will be okay. We are here with you," my mother says through tear stained eyes. It's rare to see this woman cry. So trust me when I say, my dad and I are in shock. This lesson is no joke. As soon as I get this taken care of, getting an IUD is first on my list. I need to refocus and prioritize what is important in life. I know I have a good head on my shoulders. I should have known to never trust a big dick and a smile.

Scheduling the termination of my pregnancy was not a phone call I was prepared to make. Planned parenthood asked so many probing questions, from how many sexual partners have I had, to have I had any STD's. They offered more than one option for termination. The first option was a surgical abortion and the second option was the abortion pill. My head is now spinning from all of the information. The pill seemed like the easiest and less abrasive option. I just want this to be over. Even after the appointment was set, I weighed the pros and cons. Do I really want to be someone's mother? Can I handle raising this child alone? I can't help but think about how kids are expensive. I don't even take care of myself.

Eventually, after the appointment was made, Al came over. But the conversation quickly turned into an argument that ended whatever it was that we had.

"Al, if you wanted me to consider keeping this baby, don't you think you should have been here with me? I found out BY MYSELF. I told my parents BY MYSELF and if I keep it, I know I will be raising this damn baby BY MYSELF!" I scream.

"I have had a lot on my plate recently, that's why I haven't been around. You aren't even asking my opinion about the situation. You're just telling me what you're going to do. You didn't make the baby by yourself, and I'm damn sure not going with you to kill my fucking seed. What the fuck you thought this was?! It was no problem when I was over here digging you out, but the first bump in the road we have, you on some bullshit."

I can't lie, I'm getting scared. Dude is like… enraged. I no longer see the handsome, smooth, light skinned complexioned, clean cut man I thought I was falling in love with. His face is now red, and spit is starting to fly from his mouth.

"Look, I see this as way more than a bump in the fucking road and you obviously have lost your mind, so you need to leave. Dude, you need to get out!" I yell, my heart racing.

A sickening feeling comes over me and I push his trifling ass out of the way to run to the toilet. As I am praying to the porcelain god, I hear a loud crash and then the door slams. Once I was able to make it out of the bathroom, I see the pictures of us torn up all over the floor and a damn hole in my wall. This muthafucka! They don't make men like they used to because this is the true definition of bitchassness! After all of this my head is pounding. I have to lay down for a while.

When I lay down the sun is peeking through the blinds alerting anyone who wants to go outside to rethink that decision. The Texas heat is like no other. Completely wiped out, I wake from my slumber at going on 10:30pm. This baby has me sleeping something serious. I can't avoid my situation no matter how much I try. While I was sleeping, I dreamt of motherhood and I saw an amazing baby shower. The gathering of all of my friends and family, and the delivery of a beautiful baby girl who stole my smile filled my thoughts. Al never left my side. Our home was full of laughter and joy as my mini me grew up in a happy environment with two wonderful parents.

My phone interrupts my thoughts of what could be while I rub my stomach.

"Hello," I say, though my thoughts are still

on a baby girl. I decide I needed to go see Al right now.

"D, it's Nae. I need to talk to you ASAP," JaNae told me. "When I came over to your house . . ."

"Sweetie, I'm on a mission right now, let me call you back," I say hanging up the phone while my girl was in mid-sentence. I will get to her later. Right now, I need to hear Al out and really listen to him. Can we work this out? Was I too quick to jump to conclusions? These are the thoughts that enter my mind on the frantic drive to Al's room. He lives in a popular fraternity house that was always consumed with people. Quickly parking, I make my way through the usual party goers headed towards Al's room. Nervously, I walked toward what could be the start of forever but as I get near the room, I hear him talking to a female, so I stop and listen.

"I can't lie, when you told me you were pregnant I wasn't cool with the idea, but now the more that I think about it, I'm excited to be a father," Al says.

"Baby I knew you would come around. Nobody out here has what we have together, this was meant to be. Tell your little groupies what it really is. I'm wifey, and that's what it's going to be," she says to him.

"You're having my son and you're going to be my

wife," he tells her passionately. No longer stable enough to stand and listen to this bullshit any further, I politely step inside of his room. Tears are rolling down my face, and my heart is filled with anger because I see him kissing her very full belly.

"Is she aware that you have another kid on the way ,and you just begged me not to kill your baby?" I say, charging at him, swinging with everything I have. "You muthafucka! You ain't shit! And to think I was coming here to tell you I was keeping the baby. Never!" I yell.

I run out of his room and the bitch sitting on his bed, who looked oh-too-familiar, is laughing. My chest hurts so badly from the pain. I just need to get to my car. I can't breathe. At that very moment everything goes dark.

Chapter 12
Rhonda

I had been watching him since freshman year, just sitting back and admiring from a distance. Invisibility wore me like a warm coat, so my wondering eyes were never noticed. He went straight from a boy to a man, totally skipping the awkward phase. When he got braces he was even cuter to look at, making his then dashing smile turn to beautiful. When he began playing sports, I was at every game silently cheering him on with friends who were none the wiser.

As for myself, the ugly duckling phase hit me like a ton of bricks: thick glasses, acne, unmanageable hair, and literally no confidence. Shit started to change for me in high school. I got a job and bought contacts, went to a dermatologist to get this acne together, and finally I lived in the beauty shop. The summer heading into junior year, I made a goal and that was for him to be mine. My transformation from geek to chic was so on point that everyone thought I was new on the first day of school. I kept my style fly because I worked in the mall. I had discounts on discounts. I befriended people in the department store I worked in who could help with the transformation. With new make- up, jewelry, and clothes, honey I was on it.

Now to make him want me! I had to constantly be in his sight without being obvious. I had to pay a senior $75.00 to switch lockers with me to be three lockers away. This also allowed me to gather information on the low. I was collecting intel like I was in the C.I.A. I knew his likes and dislikes. I knew where he would be and when. All I had to do was shut up and listen. Believe me, niggas talk more than females. He was always on the phone or his boys were surrounding his locker. The killer thing about it was he wasn't the most popular dude in school, or the finest, but he was the dude for me.

It was time to put a plan in motion. Al closed his locker and started walking in my direction; I stepped in his way knowing he wasn't paying attention. Of course, he ran into me, knocking everything out of my hands.

"Hey you need to watch where you're going!" I said anticipating his next move.

"Damn baby, I'm sorry. My bad. I can't lie and say I'm mad I ran into you though," he said helping me pick up my books.

"It's alright, I guess," I said giving him that annoyed but shy role. Frantically picking up the rest of my belongings, our hands touched and he looked me deep in my eyes.

"Where are you going in such a rush beautiful?" Al really thought he was spitting game. Little did he know that I planned this little run in a week ago, down to the outfit.

"I'm trying not to miss my bus. I couldn't get a ride

home with anyone today, so I'm stuck on the bus. Got to go," I told him as I walked off slowly… 3, 2, 1.

"Hey, the least I can do in give you a ride since I damn near knocked you down. My name is Alex by the way, but everyone just calls me Al."

Got him Coach!

"I don't know you Al, and I really need to get home. Thanks though," I politely told him and then I sprinted off; also a part of my plan. I didn't want to catch the bus a bit more than a man on the moon. The parking lot was next to the bus ramp, so he couldn't miss my sad face as I "missed" the bus.

I waved my hand and yelled wait just as the bus pulled off. Out of my peripheral vision, I could see him walking to his car. My head was slightly down, but I could see him checking for me. I had on a thigh length skirt, so the baby thigh was out and the ass was sitting nice. My V-neck was starting to stick to me, which had my C cups glistening. The V-cut was purposely low enough to see them.

As he drove closer to me, he slowed down then howled.

I just smiled and said, "I guess I could use that ride after all. My name is Rhonda," I told him as I led him towards my house and we had a good little conversation.

He told me plenty of things I already knew about him. I saw a picture of him and a female on the dash, but I couldn't get a good look at it. "So who's in the picture with you?" I asked casually.

"That's my girlfriend, Kera," he said matter-of- factly. I damn near died. GIRLFRIEND! Where did this bitch come from?

"Oh really, can I see the picture? I've never seen her at school before." I needed to know where this bitch came from immediately.

"We met at camp for our church last year. She doesn't go to school with us."

Now he was going on about her and how they took a purity pledge, and my fucking head was about to explode. Thank God he pulled up to my house. I quickly said thank you and got out. I knew no one was home, so I spazzed the fuck out. A girlfriend? I did all of that for nothing. He was supposed to be mine!

"Bitch calm down," I told myself. Mom will be home and call the doctor if she sees this shit, so let's think. Trying to calm down and gain my composure, I knew that I had to hatch another plan. THINK!

As time went by, Al and I formed a friendship and I flirted with him every chance I got. At first, he wasn't feeling my advances, but he slowly came around. I had to get rid of little Ms. Goodie-Goodie.

One of the seniors threw a party, *The Party*. I knew I had to be there, and I was prepared. That night was the night I was going to get what I wanted. I just needed a little liquid courage. Me and my girls made our way to the dance floor after a few shots. Trust, I was feeling good. On the dance floor I was swaying my hips in such a sexy way that it was like a mating call. While I danced with guys left and right, I stared at Al wanting and yearning for him to come and touch me. I stared at him while he drank whatever potion was in his cup, and he finally felt my pull and came over. I was 18, and I was feeling full grown. He walked over to me.

"What do you want from me? What kind of game

are you playing with my head?" he slurred as he kissed me in the middle of the party. I could feel his manhood awaken. With a crowded party, no one could see me dancing hard enough to have him at full salute. Not able to take it any longer, he took my hand. Well prepared, I followed and behind those closed doors his purity promise was broken.

Kera was the first of many bitches to get dismissed to date and obviously not the last. Denise had a lot worse coming to her if she wouldn't have bowed out gracefully. Bitches were always trying to test me, and I was prepared to take it as far as I needed to for my man. Since Denise obviously didn't get the message with the four flats or the note I left her ass, I had more coming for her. She needed to know she wasn't running shit, and she is not the first one I had to discard. She had better ask Carmen, Tasha, Stephanie, or Sonya. Oh sorry, she can't ask Sonya. I chuckle as I think about what I did to her.

Al started seeing Sonya the summer after our senior year. I spazzed the fuck out on him constantly for not spending enough time with me and he grew tired of my unstable behavior. The most hurtful thing he ever said to me was, "I need space." Yeah, space to be with that bitch is what I told myself. In my mind, it was Sonya's fault that Al left, and she had to pay. One particular night she posted a picture on her social media accounts with the hashtag #MeAndBabeLateNiteDateNite. Her dumb ass even checked-in her location. They were at Steak 48. Dumbass gave me all the information I needed because she was an attention whore. Always all over Snap Chat and IG every five minutes with her every move. Stalking her wasn't hard at all. I knew her full name, address, birthday, and job location because she wanted the world to know. Always using those stupid ass dog filters blowing kisses at my man and shit.

Patiently, I waited for them across the street from the restaurant where I went unnoticed. Al kissed the little home wrecker eagerly and said his goodbyes. He got into his dad's black and chrome Chevrolet F-150, heading to his next destination. The more I pictured her being happy with my man, the more enraged I got. She got her keys from the valet and hopped into her gray Honda Civic heading home.

Driving 25 miles per hour or so from the restaurant, she neared Northeast Houston and headed down a very dark and twisted street in East Mount Houston. I had a plan. I pulled up on her erratically, swerving in and out of the lanes with my bright lights on, which blinded her. That way she couldn't recognize my vehicle. She was trying to avoid me, which caused her to lose control of the car. All it took was a nice hit to her bumper to send her flying off of the road, down the hill, and into a tree.

The vehicle contained OnStar, which alerted 911, but by the time the paramedics found her, she was unconscious from the impact of accident. Sonya flew through the windshield and landed on the hood of the vehicle. She ended up having multiple lacerations on the right side of her face. That ended that little love affair before it really got started. Al is all about image and ol' Scarface didn't exactly fit the mold anymore. I have to say, that was some of my best work! I kept trying to tell these bitches to stop trying me!

The best part is that Al has no idea. He thinks I am his sweet, or shall I say naïve, little girlfriend. Honey, I've had trackers on his phone and car since we first started dating. He can't cut a step without me knowing.

That's how I know how to find and take care of these females.

Now that I'm pregnant, I haven't been able to take my mood stabilizers out of concern for the baby and I am afraid he will find out. When I was 13, I was diagnosed with Bipolar Disorder. My mood swings vary from feeling overly happy or outgoing, to an extremely irritable mood with extreme agitation. My mother is the only person who can connect with me and calm me down when I'm having an episode, and I don't need her trying to check me into the hospital, so the less she knows the better. Al can never find out.

Chapter 13
Denise

When I wake up, I have no idea what's going on, and I see worried faces around the room. Where am I? Why is mommy crying?

"What's going on?" I muster enough energy to say through an extremely dry throat.

"My baby! Lord Jesus, thank you," my father says. Now I'm really confused. The more I look around, things become less foggy.

"You're in a hospital. There are some things we need to tell you. Can everyone step out while we talk to Denise?" my mother asks.

Bri, Nae, my brother, and some of my sorors leave the room. What is my brother doing here? Walt lives all the way in Dallas, which is four hours away.

"Baby, do you remember anything that happened before you passed out?" Mom asks.

"No ma'am, not really. How did I even get here mom?" I ask. Damn my head is pounding. This is really starting to scare me.

"You were brought here by the ambulance. You passed out at a frat house on campus. People said you were fighting with the baby's father and as you were leaving, you passed out. Someone then called 911," my father explains. "That son of a bitch!"

"Please, calm down Harold."

"Wait," I say, "I do remember going to see Al....my baby! How is my baby?" I ask rubbing my stomach. "I decided to keep it yesterday. I know it will not be easy, but I can do it."

My parents look at each other with uneasy faces. Tears begin to roll down my mom's face, which worries me since this is the second time, in a matter of days, I have seen her cry.

"Baby, since you were admitted, testing shows that during your pregnancy you had blood preeclampsia and high blood pressure, which I'm sure you know is dangerous."

"Oh my God yes. Are they helping to bring my pressure down so that it doesn't affect the baby? This is serious. We studied about it in class. That explains why I have been so dizzy lately," I say, thinking back on the past few weeks.

"When they brought you in, your blood pressure was through the roof. You were on the edge of having a stroke. You had to have emergency surgery. I'm so sorry, they did everything they could, but the baby just wasn't strong enough yet. The baby didn't make it." My mom looks at me and covers her mouth as I stare at her in silence.

"Okay, wait. I said I was keeping the baby. I saw her.

I had a dream, and she was beautiful. This can't be right. Mommy! Daddy! Please, please say this is not real! I'm getting out of here!" I try to yank out the IVs they have in my arm. I start yelling and screaming for them to let me the hell out of here. My friends and family start to come back into the room, trying to figure out what is going on and telling me to calm down and that it will be okay. Yet I can't calm down. How can I really, when I no longer have my baby girl?

"I have to tell Al," I say, which instantly sends the room into a frenzy, and I can't blame one single person for being upset. He is public enemy #1. My brother is pissed more than anyone. Walt has always been a very protective big brother, and we were very close. Our birthdays are three years and one day apart. His is January 3rd and mine is January 4th. The resemblance is uncanny, so we always call each other "Twin."

"I saw him and tried to beat the brakes off his ass. You fuck with my sister, you fuck with me!" Walt says through clenched teeth. Things are starting to come back to me now. I remembered Al kissing the girl on her belly because she was pregnant and confessing his love to her. I was still trying to figure out who she was. While I was working that out in my head, my nurse came in telling everyone they need to go into the waiting area because I'm too upset. She inserts a mild sedative into my IV, and I quickly slip away. Lord, please let me see my baby girl again.

A time of crisis is when you see what you mean to others. There are get well balloons and flowers everywhere. My visitors list goes on for pages as loved ones continue showing concern and care. They have literally loved me back to myself. I have to spend two more days in the hospital. At first, I just wanted to have a pity party and cry, but I have come back around. I had to, at least for my own sanity. God doesn't make mistakes, and everything happens for a reason. This just isn't my time. I will be blessed in the future and will have a loving family. Being in that circus with Al would have been a world of trouble and grief. I have to make better decisions for myself going forward. My heart is still hurting, but I am making my peace with the situation.

Even after my release from the hospital, I can't say that I feel alone. My parents, Bri, Chase, Nae, and Walt continue to care for me until I am mentally and physically able to care for myself. I am beyond thankful for them. I know, in time, the pain will hurt a little bit less. But, it's time to get back out into this world. Going through this ordeal, I learned so much about the female body, and I'm thinking heavily about switching from pediatric nursing to gynecology. I won't lose any school credits, but I will be in school longer. Still, if I can help one woman to avoid the pain I felt, it will be worth it. Man, how things have changed. I have been in the house way too long, with too much on my brain. I have cabin fever, so I'm breaking out this weekend. It is about time to hit the salon, nail shop, and the mall and I am determined to help my girls get this poetry night together. It's the least I can do since they have been here for me around the clock.

Chapter 14
JaNae

The time has come for our first *Psi Kapp Poetry Night*. As neos, we have to show that our ideas are taking the sorority in the right direction, or they will be pushed along the wayside if Candice has anything to do with it. I personally don't believe in that dictatorship bullshit. We didn't join this sorority for that. Poetry night is about bringing in revenue, shining a positive light on our chapter, and contributing to the community. Twenty percent of the proceeds are going to M.D. Anderson Hospital for cancer patients. We chose them because cancer has affected all of our lives in one way or another. Sororities are not just about having parties. The main goal is to serve the community.

The venue for the event holds 65-75 people comfortably. We plan on filling every seat with performers, poets, poetry lovers, and supporters. This has definitely been a group effort. I am leading the event, but none of this would be possible if all delegated responsibilities were not completed. A leader is nothing without a good team. I am a business major, so I am making sure that I have business portion down pat. Now, I never thought of it before, but this event has made me think about doing event planning as a career. Can I do this for a living? Let me see, use other people's money to plan fabulous parties and events. Hell yeah, I can do it. I'm going to research that first thing tomorrow.

For now, I'm running down a nearly completed checklist. The décor is completed, eye popping, yet not over the top. The chapter's treasurer and secretary are at the door to handle all funds. The DJ is on deck. I am so glad we were able to get DJ No- Malice, who has been killing it all over town. I know he will draw a crowd. All thanks go to Denise for the hook up. We have asked six of the sisters to be sexy waitresses to serve the crowd some eye candy. Their faces are beat to the gods and the uniforms set it off. We decided on black bustier tops, ripped jeans, and heels with huge blinged out necklaces hitting their cleavage in just the right places. The girls are definitely on point. The money made at bar belonged to the venue, but the tips belonged to the girls, so they will make sure to keep the people happy. It's yet another great detail about this event.

To my surprise, Denise joins Bri in coming to check on me before the doors open and we can get things started. After everything she has been through, it is so good to see my girl up and out.

"Nae, I have the local black newspaper and the college collegiate paper on deck," Bri informs me. "Denise, you did a great job setting things up

with the venue and the DJ. It is so much more than expected and one less thing on my back. I just don't want any of the sisters to have any reason to talk shit about our event," I admit.

"No matter what, we've got you as always. So, stop stressing and go host this show. I still can't believe you are not going to hit the mic yourself, but hey, no pressure…pleeeease?" Denise pouted.

"Girl gone. Let's do one last check. I'm going to call all of the poets to the back, and we're going to roll with it. While I'm hosting, please look out for any other problems that may occur with sorors, the door, poets, or servers." I'm such a drill sergeant.

"Got it Boss! We've been planning this for too long. Chase and one of his boys are coming too," Bri said smiling.

"Bri, y'all are such a cute little couple. I'm so happy for you. He is such a cool person and I appreciate the fact that he came with you to visit me. He gets my respect for that," Denise says, looking off slightly. "Okay, we are not gonna start crying in here, so I'm gonna let it go for now."

"Hey, the more the merrier, right? I'll holla at him later for sure. Thank you again for all of your hard work. We're about to kill it." Hugging all my girls, I let them go to do other prep work.

I walk back to the main stage area and, to my surprise, the room is already over fifty percent full. That's what I'm talking about. Finally, I can see it all coming together. Kelly hands me the sign in sheet for poets, which is full and has two extras on the bottom. I see the poets are definitely in the house.

"Good evening good people. My name is *Poetic Justice* and we would like to welcome you to our first *Purple and Gold Poetry Night.* Give it up! Yes! We wanted to give the city's finest an outlet to get busy on the mic. Now, we have signature drinks and beautiful waitresses walking around here to get you those beverages. Let's not forget to tip the ladies though. As they say, the bigger the tip the bigger the sip. There is also a kitchen, so make your orders, get ya hot sauce out ya bag-SWAG! Now, let me get all the poets to the back, and I'm going to leave you with DJ No-Malice. Let's get it!"

I meet up with the poets to let them know to bring the energy. Don't do more than two pieces at a time and keep it moving. Many of the poets are asking if this is going to be a regular thing. Of course that depends on how tonight turns out. I like the demographic of poets because no one looks the same and everyone is cool. We say a quick prayer, and now it is time for the show.

The room is jumping and the music is live. The bar is full and people are still walking in as I step to the mic.

"Alright *Poetic Justice* back at cha. Y'all ready for a good time? Say yeah!"

"Yeah!" the crowd screams.

"When you hear something you like, you snap.

Snap along with me." The crowd starts snapping. "No booing or disturbing the artist. We must

respect the mic. If you agree, let me hear you say 'Yeah.' First…coming to the stage, we have Mizz Monday!"

Mizz Monday let it be known that she is more than a baby momma escaping hood politics and antics. Artist after artist gave it up on the stage. Some of them I'd seen in passing, and I had no clue they were even artists. The first half of the set goes great, or so I think. To my left side sits a table with our chapter sorors and sorors from visiting chapters. I can see a scowl on Candice's face. What is the bitch tripping on now? I know I'll get an earful later. Her evil ass keeps mean mugging me.

Next thing I know, Bri is politely escorting her ass out. My dog! To the right, I see Al's hoe ass walking inside. He can't be serious. I'm not going to make a scene at our function, and hopefully Denise won't either. Think fast Nae. I know what to do. I get back on the stage and give the DJ the cut music sign. I start talking to the crowd again.

"Alright, alright we're back. I hope y'all are enjoying yourselves. We've had some amazing artists to bless the stage. Give 'em another round of applause!"

I can see Denise about to go off on this asshole, and we don't need this drama. Not tonight.

"My girls Denise and Bri asked me to bless the mic and even though I wasn't going to, hey, why not? You want me to drop a little something on y'all?!"

I know hearing her name will stop Denise dead in her tracks. Bri mouths thank you as she stands next to her Chase, and standing beside him is James, AKA Mr. Eastcoast. Now this is a shocker. So, James is the friend that was coming with Chase. Well damn!

"Like Erykah, I'm an artist and I'm sensitive about my shit. Here we go. This piece is called *Not Another Secret.*"

> *I hate being a secret!*
>
> *A torrid love affair to be kept within my bedroom walls or the walls of my mind*
>
> *Damn, we running out of time*
>
> *Like Cinderella, you can't stay past midnight even if the mood is right*
>
> *Since you gotta run home to the love of yo life LOVE, my ass! If you loved her so much you wouldn't be craving my touch*
>
> *And you wouldn't call me when "she" fuck up*
>
> *It's funny how you working hard trying to maintain both households*
>
> *Why do I miss you when the right side of my bed gets cold*
>
> *Does she do it like me? Does she unleash you inner most fantasies*
>
> *No pressure here, we trade pain for pleasure in our world*
>
> *Far from your woman, but I'm a very freaky girl*

*Damn, I'm wanting more and more
of your time*

Wishing you were mine

*You know how to make me feel
good, which I knew you would*

*These feelings I got are misunder-
stood*

*You're getting in my head, this was
supposed to end at the bed*

*I don't catch warm fuzzy feelings
That shit now is dead*

*Didn't read the fine print where it
said Keep ya head in check*

Yet, it's beyond the sex

*I been here before, hittin' rendezvous
spots on the low*

*Too much at stake for anyone to
find out, no one can know*

*This will not turn out well, how long
can I do this*

*Caught up with you as I think to
myself*

Not another secret

Once I finish, snaps and applause erupt all over the room. Looking in Denise's direction, I notice a single tear slip down her cheek as she claps her hands. She comes over to give me a hug, telling me thank you and letting me know she loves me. It isn't a shocker that Al left before my piece was finished. I was shooting slugs directly at his ass. The second set of the show flies by. I notice eyes on me the whole time but pretend not to notice.

"I want to thank y'all for coming out on behalf of the Purple and Gold. If you want us to bring poetry night back, let it be known on social media. Thank y'all for coming out, goodnight!"

It is finally over, and things went well. I really hope to make my chapter proud. We made $450 at the door between admissions and donations, the girls were getting great tips, and each poet was amazing. I couldn't have dreamt of a better night.

"Yo ma. I didn't know you had it like that. I don't know who pissed you off, but you went in on their ass! I said, 'Yo, look at shorty'," James says, smiling the whole time.

"Had to send a message, but I'm glad you liked it. I didn't know you were cool with Chase," I say being nosy.

"Yeah, Chase is my boy. We're roommates," he says. Ain't this a bitch? I been trying to find out about dude all this time, and he was right under my nose. The irony of it all. I wonder why Bri didn't know. Maybe Chase was always in her room. James sits and talks with me for a while. I can't lie, it does feel nice to get a little male attention. I must say he is cool as hell, plus he is crazy funny. Lord, those pretty ass teeth and east coast swag are killing me. I make sure we exchanged phone numbers so we could see where things can go from here. There is no way I am letting him get away this time.

Chapter 15
James

Running into JaNae was a pleasant surprise for ya boy, I can't even front. I also can't ignore the fact that there is something between us. She has me intrigued. It's unfamiliar territory, but I'm willing to look into it. Usually females don't hold my attention past a hook up, but this is not the same. JaNae knows how to hold a conversation and keep me interested. I can't find anything wrong with beauty and brains.

The way shorty got on the mic to spit that poem really blew me away. The way she said every line with feeling and punch lines that would crack the face of any adversary showed me that she was more than just your average chic. 1 wouldn't put her in the same category as all of the one-nighters I'm used to dealing with. Fuckin' a lot of girls was cool, but sometimes that shit gets old. These days, women don't make you work for it, so I feel no need to lead anybody on or lie to them. If you look clingy or thirsty in the slightest bit, I'm not with it. There is no need for the unnecessary drama. I keep shit easy around my way.

Being from Jersey, my way of thinking is a bit different than the fellas that I'm cool with down here in the dirty south. My swag is even different, something you either have or you don't. An outfit or a car never made me and whether I have on a white tee, fitted jeans, and some Timbs or a suit my confidence speaks for me without me having to say a word. I turn heads without even speaking.

Things people don't know about me is the fact that I graduated in the top 10 of my class and I am here for a full ride on an academic scholarship. Don't let the way I dress and my nonchalant demeanor fool you. I sit back and peep the scene while other niggas are running their mouths. I had to learn that shit at an early age. The ones that niggas rolled up on first was the ones talking the loudest. I'm more of the chill guy. No need to boast, that's how you bring unnecessary heat in your direction.

As a kid, my mom always had a dope boy for a boyfriend. She refused to want for anything or for us to be on welfare. So, that's how she kept that extra dough flowing in the house. My mom was a hair stylist with a full salon in the basement. Also, from time to time, the knuckle headed boyfriends of hers would do dirt down there. Keeping the hood on lock, all of her clients rocked the newest and the latest styles. Grooming me at a young age with those clippers, I couldn't wait until I was a little older to get my own chair beside her. In my household, you had to hustle. After the age of 12, you were considered grown and needed to make your own money. Since the clippers were my first hustle, I was able to afford the extras like Jordans and jerseys when mom wasn't shelling out that dough.

I cut five to six heads a week, and at 15 I was my own boss; I was still humble though. That's one thing that my father taught me. He would say, "When these boys were out here shining for the world to see, and bragging about what they had, it is always somebody watching or hatin' that's trying to come up." That's a lesson I will never forget. My older sister, Tiffany, worked up the block at a bodega to get her ends while she was in community college.

Our pops was sentenced to life in prison for running a drug cartel, so he calls Rikers Island his home. Growing up, visits were few-and-far between and, as I got older, we were able to keep in touch online. He isn't denied access to much. He has a way around everything. He's treated like a king in and out of lock up. But even though people knew him, he was more like a ghost in my house. James Rovell Sr's name will always carry weight in our neighborhood. Even now, if he says the words, your ass will get touched.

Slim was mom's last boyfriend. His aura alone said he wasn't shit. This muthafucka thought he was about to come in and run shit, but the last straw for me was when I saw this nigga making eyes at my sister and slapping her on the ass as she walked by and she had the nerve to giggle. Her being eighteen or not, that shit was not about to go down.

"Man don't touch my sister! What the fuck is wrong with you?" I pushed Slim away from Tiffany with force and bucked up to his ass to let him know I was ready to put in work if need be.

"Lil nigga this my house, and you ain't shit. I pay the bills in this mufucka! I was just playing with her ass anyway. Sit yo punk ass down before I sit you down," Slim said while raising up his T-shirt that exposed a chrome 9 Millimeter. That's the type of punk ass nigga he was.

"Jay, come on let's go. It ain't worth it. Don't do something stupid," Tiffany begged, trying to pull me out of the room.

"Hell no! Who the fuck does he think he is? I promise, this ain't the end of this homeboy!" I told him. This bitch blew a kiss at me like it was nothing. He was about to learn the hard way.

I don't know what the hell my moms saw in his shady, bottom of the barrel ass. He was known for cheating people out of product and the streets didn't have any positive shit to say about dude. It was time to put a plan in action to get rid of him. I contacted my pop's people because it was time to get busy. When I said my pops was connected, it was no joke. Even though my mother moved on with her life, he still looked out for us, especially since he had been on the inside. He had eyes all over. We were always told that if we ever needed anything to contact Big Will, my pop's right hand. I was definitely hitting him up to come handle this fool.

After I got out of school the following day I was going to sit down with my mom and Big Will so we could come up with a solution to get Slim out of the house for good. Either that, or Big Will and his goons would show him the way out the hard way. Entering the crib, everything felt still. It was way too quiet, as if no one was home. Any other time there was all kinds of noise and chaos going on from my mom's clients and their kids, to Slim and his lame ass boys. I headed down the stairs to speak to my mom, but the stairs were so slippery that I fell on the steps. "What the hell?" I yelled trying to get up so I

could turn on the light.

I didn't know if mom wasted hair products on the steps or what. Finally reaching the light after slipping and sliding, I wished I'd never come down stairs. The scene will forever be etched in my mind. Three bodies lying on the floor lifeless. My mother, Tiffany, and Slim. Shaking my mother and sister, I yelled and cried for them to get up, but neither of them did as I requested. They both had gunshot wounds to the chest. Slim's throat was cut and his tongue was cut out, laying on the floor beside him. He was stripped of all his jewels, and the safe that he kept downstairs was open and emptied.

Someone killed my family and stole Slim's stash. Because of this slimy muthafucka, my family paid the ultimate price. The news reported it as a drug dealer slain and there was no mention of my loved ones; just another senseless act of black-on- black crime is what viewers saw on the news. They were gone, and I was 15 and alone.

After the burial, my grandparents brought me down south to Houston. And, since I was new to the city, no one was close enough to me to affect me by coming or going in and out of my life. I didn't allow it. Yet, I meet JaNae and she is all I can think about, which makes me crazy uncomfortable. Should I let her into my world?

Chapter 16
Brianna

The last few months have been a blur. Since the cotillion, my phone hasn't stopped ringing and I have been booking jobs left and right. The events have included phenomenal pay, so I am able to finally move out of the dorms and pay my rent up for the next six months. I am well aware that there is no guarantee with dance, so when you get a check you have to take care of business first and ball out later.

I took the summer off from school to focus on my career since I've been blessed with so many opportunities. Next semester will be no joke. With a major in business and a minor in dance, I decided to apply for an accelerated program to graduate early to keep growing my brand. There is no way I'm quitting school, but at least I can hurry this process along. Plus, my mommy and daddy would kill me. They raised me and Daja to take care of business by any means necessary, but nothing is to get in the way of our education.

After three business meetings and presentations for *The Southern Gospel Explosion, Creole Summer Jam,* and *Wine*

Fest 2018 in Houston and Dallas, your girl is ready to call it a day. I just want to sit back chill for a moment. I haven't seen my honey in a few days, so I'm definitely in need of some QT.

I get off of the elevator and head to my apartment when I notice a note attached to the door: *Welcome home. Do not be alarmed by anything you see inside these doors. Just relax and enjoy. -Chase*

Hmmm, okay. I unlock the door and hear Prince singing "Adore", one of my favorite songs. I walk through the apartment and there is a masseuse setting up her table in the living room and a hibachi chef setting up in my kitchen. What in the world does this man have going on in my house?

"Good evening Ms. Brianna. My name is Pam. I will be your masseuse for the evening. Your bath has already been drawn and immediately afterward you will return to my area for a massage. Please follow me."

This woman, who I don't know, is leading me through my home. As we reached the beautiful bathroom, which has now been filled with lilies and roses, there is a bubble bath and another note that reads:

Please enjoy the bath and massage. You deserve to be pampered. Your hard work doesn't go unnoticed. You take care of everyone else, now let me take care of you. —Chase

My eyes begin to water as I think to myself, *I didn't do anything for recognition. I did the best I could with what was put in front of me.* Being in a loving relationship has my mind blown. Chase has managed to climb over walls and cut through the barbed wire surrounding my heart.

Pam excuses herself so I can get undressed. Doing as I was asked, I soak in my garden tub for the first time since I moved in, and it does feel nice to be pampered.

Once I finish with my luxurious milk bath, I begin to dry off when a knock on the door startles me.

"Yes," I answer.

"Ms. Brianna, may I come in?" Pam asks.

"Yes. You may."

"Here is your attire for your massage and a glass of wine."

"Well, thank you Pam. I will be out in a moment," I inform her. The wine was chilled to perfection. This man is pulling out all the stops.

I step out of the bathroom and onto a bed of rose petals that lead me back to the massage table. Aromatherapy candles and bouquets of roses surround my living room. Dressed in the robe and panties that Pam left for me, I head to the massage table that is hidden behind a partition.

"Ms. Brianna, I am Chef Thomas and here are your hors d'oeuvres. Enjoy," Chef Thomas says, placing a plate of four sushi rolls in front of me.

"Thank you so much! I love sushi." I didn't realize that I was so busy today that I really hadn't eaten much. The fruit smoothie and a bagel I had for breakfast were totally gone. I take a bite and the sushi is delicious. Chef made California Rolls with grilled shrimp and avocado, and they are so flavorful.

After leaving half of a piece of the sushi on the plate, I finished up my glass of wine and then prepared to relax for my massage.

"Ms. Brianna, please hand me your robe and lay on the table," Pam instructs as she stands by the table with a sheet in hand to lie on top of me.

"Just relax," she says.

Pam melted all of the tension and strain out of my shoulders, arms, back, legs, and feet. I have to say a silent prayer of thanks for these wonderful gifts. I lay there for what feels like hours until I doze off.

Gently waking me out of my sleep, Pam let me know that she is finished. Through my speakers, Nivea was letting her man know 25 reasons why she loved him. The aroma of the food Chef Thomas is cooking is making my stomach growl.

"Good night Ms. Brianna. Here you go," Pam says as she hands me a sexy, long satin gown with a slit up my thigh and another note that reads:

I hope you enjoyed part one. Please join me for part two. - Chase

He is way too much. I thank Pam for all that she has done, and I feel like I am floating on a cloud. Placing the gown on, the satin feels so sexy as it falls over my body. The parts that it's covering, my C cups are sitting up nice. Sliding on my black pumps, I complete my outfit for my dinner reservation. I put a little Michael Kors perfume behind each ear and head out to see my man.

I walk only a few steps into my dining room and there he stands, looking as handsome as he wants to look. His fresh fade and edge up is on point and his Polo V-neck, jeans, and LV tennis shoes are clean. When I say this GQ man is looking delicious, PLEASE BELIEVE ME! He must have been thinking the same about me because the look on his face is priceless.

"Damn baby! You look beautiful. Come here girl." He bends down to kiss my lips and ignites a fire within me.

I manage to say, "Thank you, love. Thank you for all

of this. How did you pull all of this together?"

"Just know I had a team of people. Now let's sit down and eat. Let me feed you," he says in a cocky tone.

Pulling out my chair, he helps me sit me at the table. I make sure to have my entire thigh out by crossing my legs, making that split come up to my hip.

"I see you babe, don't think I don't see you," he says, shaking his head. Chef Thomas brings over salads and ten minutes later the main course. Grilled chicken and lobster over fried rice with extra garlic butter, my favorite meal. After the food is placed in front of us, the chef exits quietly.

"Baby, you are too much. I just can't believe you did all of this," I say, teary eyed.

"I'm not giving you things you don't deserve. Just stick with ya boy. This is only the beginning. I wish I could call all your exes and personally thank them for fucking up, so I could get the woman of my dreams. I know what I have, and I needed you to see what we have. This is not a game to me. I want you to be here with me through the good and the bad. Baby, I support all that you do, I see your name in lights because of your talents. People also want to be surrounded by your goodness. I know I'm blessed to be here."

Tears are rolling down my face because all of this was so unexpected. "I have a confession," I say. "I have been staying busy to avoid dealing with my feelings for you. I knew from the first day I saw you again that I was in trouble. Fear made my heart unavailable for so long that I didn't know how to react," I confessed.

"Baby, don't be scared of me or us. I love you, and I'm not going anywhere," he says as he gently rubs my face.

Standing up, I walk over to him and kiss him long and hard, whispering in his ear, "I love you, too."

After moving the plates to the side, Chase picks me up and sits me on the table. Kissing me passionately down the right side of my neck, he slides my gown strap down, exposes my nipple, and begins sucking and licking hungrily. Raising my gown from the bottom, Chase looks at my very pretty, Brazilian waxed little lady.

"Can I taste you?" he asks, licking his lips. "You can do more than that."

Feeling some kind of way, I slide my thong to the side so my clit is now free. Taking my middle finger, I rotate it in a circular motion, giving me complete arousal. The only sound I can hear is my soft whimpers and the sounds of my wetness. As if on cue, Chase licks my pierced hood and literally tastes me. Looking at me with approval while licking his lips, he scoots me to the edge of the table like a doctor preparing a patient for an exam. Yet, he is preparing for much more. I lean back onto my elbows, and my heels are wrapped around his back for a deeper feel.

This is not a game for him. This man is sucking and licking as if he knows me from a previous life. Our intensity for each other is absolutely inevitable. How has he become so acquainted with what I thought was mine? He is showing me she is now his. Without my permission, she confirms she is his as well. He gently puts me on all fours to get a different angle, an angle that I had never experienced. I'm feeling the same way as he picks me up off the table and carries me to my bed to make love to me.

I had no idea life could be like this. Someone actually gives a damn about my feelings and what makes me happy. He isn't about the take, take, take, and this is a lifestyle I can get used to having. We will have to reschedule the dinner.

Chapter 17
Denise

Summer, where have you been all my life? I'm not completely free from school, but two classes are better than four to five any day. There are no sorority meetings or community service projects because everyone has gone home. I have nothing but free time and built up frustration. What better way than take it out at the gym? The thing I love about the gym I belong to is that they offer a variety of classes. Cycling, Aqua Fit, Kickboxing. You name it, and they pretty much have something for everyone, including dance and cardio. Cherri, my trainer, suggested a fun Hip Hop class for me, Bri, and Nae for our next outing which was scheduled on my birthday. I don't just look at Cherri as my trainer but also a friend, so I invited her to hang with us too. I can't wait for Bri and Nae to meet her.

Today's Hip Hop class is a twerking workshop. The instructor teaches you a sassy booty shaking routine for the 60-minute class. I have always wanted to try it, and it looks fun. I'm so glad my girls are free to join me.

Anytime we can get together is guaranteed to be a good time.

"Ladies, I want to introduce you to Cherri," I tell them.

"Nice to finally meet you," Bri says.

"Hey girl," says Nae.

Cherri gives everyone a brief hug and then we all began to stretch it out. The instructor comes in extremely hyped and wearing a headset.

"Ladies and gentlemen, I want to see asses wiggling and booties shaking."

Taylor is our Twerk Guide for the day and she is full of life, so we all have to laugh. Taylor throws on Travis Porter's "Bring it Back" to get us going. There is nothing to be done to this song but booty shake. Honey, some of these men are in here twerking better than me, but it's all in good fun. Taylor gives us some basic movements step by step, then we put it all together. Awwwww shit, why is Rhianna's and Chris Brown's "Birthday Cake" next on the play list? That just got my crew turned up even more. I'm cool with dance moves, but hey I can move this ass a little bit. It's my birthday, but you know Bri is out there having the time of her life.

"Get it Bri," I say, sweating and trying to keep up.

"I see we have a celebrity in the house everybody. Brianna, come on up here girl and show us what you're working with!" our instructor prompted.

We all urge her to go up there. When the music comes on, Bri is a totally different beast. Lord, these heifers start having a twerk off. Asses are shaking everywhere, and after a few minutes we all join in on the fun. Learning the next routine flies right out the window. We're all free-styling and having a great time, just living life. These are the moments that I cherish most. After the workshop ends, I invite everybody over for drinks. I know I need to cool down, plus I make the best *Pink Panties* if you let my girls tell it.

"You know you make them the best D," Bri says, laughing so hard she is bursting at the seams. She's laughing because she knows that's how she can get me to make whatever she wants. My cool ass used to fall for it every time too. What can I say? I'm a sucker for a compliment. Now when she uses the old, "You make it the best" line, I just side eye her ass and then make it anyway.

"All that dancing made me hungry. Anybody want wings?" JaNae asks.

"Now you know I need some lemon pepper wings in my life," I say.

"Let's all put 10 bucks in and get a family pack. Cherri, ante up boo, and welcome to the family," Bri adds.

At the house, I'm mixing the drinks and singing loud. My K. Michelle mix is going hard on my playlist. Nae selects a family pack that includes four flavors of wings, ranch, blue cheese, carrots, and celery. The lemon pepper hot, regular lemon pepper, garlic parmesan, and bar-b-que wings smell so good they have our mouths salivating.

Bri, Nae, Cherri, and I start going in on that food like there is no tomorrow. Nobody is worried about watching their figures, or being ladylike, because we are just doing us; real friends telling stories, cracking jokes, and enjoying each other's company. This is why I like having this group of people around me. Creating true friendships with females is not easy, and keeping them for many years and through several life changes is even harder. A few hours later we start wrapping up our Iyanla Vanzant moment.

"I'm so glad we got to chill tonight. My damn voice is hoarse from singing and laughing with you fools. Cherri, you fit right in girl. Let me get out of here with my tired ass," JaNae says as she starts cleaning up before she leaves.

"Girl, I got it. Thank you for staying. Love you!" "Nae, let me catch a ride. I'm headed out too.

I didn't know I was a celebrity, but you know I'll take it heeeeeeeeeeeeey. As long as I'm getting those coins, I'll be that. I need to post that twerk session from earlier. We'd have thousands of dudes trying to follow me for sure," Bri laughs.

"Hell, you need to do PR for me so I can get more clients. Girl, you are blowing up. Hood famous!" Cherri teases. We all fall out laughing.

"I'm going to the restroom, and then I'm going to head home too," Cherri says.

"Alright girl, I'm going to walk them outside,"

I say.

While walking my crew outside, we laugh a little bit more and they head on out. It is crazy how much we have been through together. I wouldn't go through all of this shit with anybody else though. They are my bitches for life.

I walk back into the apartment to straighten up and chill and hear water running from the kitchen faucet.

"Girl, you don't have to do that. You're a guest," I say,

frowning at Cherrie as I walk in the kitchen.

"It's no problem. I just want to help, since you were kind enough to invite me over," she says.

"Damn, we did make a bit of a mess, huh? On second thought, thank you."

Getting to know her outside of the gym is cool. As we clean up, we had a few more drinks and laughed some more.

"Denise, I'm going to get out of your hair. I had a great time with you and your friends," Cherri says while picking up her purse and phone and heading to the door.

"It was no problem. You always come through for me when I need to burn this energy off, and you listen to all my craziness. It's the least I could do," I say while giving her a hug.

As I pull away, she kisses me! Not on the cheek, but on the lips. Ummm, what was that about? When she steps back, I have a look of shock on my face that cannot be concealed.

"I'm sorry, I thought we were vibing. I didn't mean any harm. Damn, I'm sorry. I had too many drinks, and I took things the wrong way," Cherri reacts nervously.

As I stand here, I can only touch my lips in shock. I had no clue she was gay.

"Do it again," I tell her. Why not, you only live once right?

"I can't believe I messed up our friendship. Wait… what?" she asks.

"Try it again," I say, somewhat nervous because I have never been in a situation like this before.

Liquid courage is a muthafucka. Smiling, Cherri

steps closer to me and kisses me softly while stroking my cheek. Allowing my inhibitions to run free, I open my mouth and allow her tongue inside as it dances alongside mine.

I wasn't expecting this at all, but I can say Cherri made it less uncomfortable with her gentleness. My mind is yelling, *What the fuck???!!!* But, my body is reacting to it. I pull away because I have to ask some questions.

"Lucy, you got some explaining to do," I say in my best Ricky Ricardo impersonation. We both laugh as we walk over to the couch. Cherri explains that she looked at me differently maybe five sessions into our training and the way my body was toning up didn't hurt either.

"I'm professional with my job, so I don't date clients. That's why I keep things strictly business."

"Until now?" I giggle with my left eyebrow up.

"Yes, until now. Like I said, blame it on the alcohol. If I was in my right mind, I never would have come at you like that."

"Oh really," I say as if I was clutching my pearls. "No, no… You're beautiful. On any given day,

I would approach you. You know what I mean, hell."

I'm weak as I watch her explain herself. Guys never do this. They don't show you that they are nervous or shy. I find it sweet and endearing.

"Sorry, you made that too easy, and thank you for saying that I'm beautiful. Another thing… I had no idea that you were gay."

"I wouldn't consider myself gay because I have been in relationships with men and women, sometimes with both at the same time. I'm just me. I look at a person's spirit, not what's in their pants. The more I got to know you, the more I saw it wasn't just your exterior, but your inner beauty. When I came to see you at the hospital, it hurt my heart to know what you were going through, because you didn't deserve that. I wanted to hold you and protect you from the world, but I couldn't. It wasn't my place. So, I just said silent prayers for you in hopes that I would get my friend back."

Just the mention of the baby, as well as hearing her thoughts concerning me made me feel some kind of way. Refusing to get over-emotional about everything, I quickly wipe my eyes.

"I'm not ready for a relationship. But, I am intrigued," I confess.

"I'm here to take you on this journey if you will allow me. Not to scare you, turn you out, or make you some flaming lesbian. That's not my thing," she says between kisses.

Kissing her is so much softer than kissing a guy. Her kisses slowly move from my lips to my neck. She stays there, focused as if she can feel the heat rising from my pores. Did she have a road map to my body? I guess it is true when they say a woman knows what another woman likes.

"Let me know if you don't like something or you are uncomfortable, okay?" I nod in response because my mind was still blown from the scene. She removes my tank top, and my Pink Victoria's Secret sports bra holds the D's in place. Off goes Victoria and the trail of kisses are now roaming all over my breasts. She holds them as she gently sucks and nibbles at the same time, and moans of pleasure escape my mouth. I've been in this situation countless times with men, but this is totally different. Cherri is now reaching for the tie on my gray sports shorts, looking up to get the go ahead from me.

"Don't know if I'm ready for that part," I tell her honestly.

"That's fine. Can I touch it?" she asks softly.

Again I nod, now a bit more nervous than before. Reaching into my panties, she touches my ever so wet ocean. Something every man I was ever with always wanted more of because they were in literal disbelief of how wet it gets.

"You are so lucky that all I can do is touch," she says, smiling and licking her lips. Back up to my breasts, her mouth covers my left nipple while her left hand gently tugs on my breast and her right hand…oh, that right hand has a party going on in my panties. She has two fingers in while her thumb is making motions and stroking my clitoris. The slow motion and anticipation of what's to come is sheer agony. She knows exactly which buttons to push. She knows when to slow down and when to speed up. The fire between my thighs ignites my entire body. My God… I take it as long as I can before exploding all over her hand. I squeeze her arm and let out a squeal even I didn't recognize. I thought that it was over, so I can catch my breath, but she keeps going faster and faster.

"Please stop… I can't take any more," I plead as she ignores my cries. Continuing with this torture, I come again and again. I was now damn near squirming off the couch until I feel another orgasm and release at the same time. I squirt all over the place. Her shirt is wet as hell when she gets up. My head is spinning. I'm in disbelief of what happened.

"Wow, I didn't expect that," she teases.

"Dudes have been trying to get me to squirt for years. It seems like you did it in ten minutes. Ain't this some shit," I say as I kiss her and then head to the shower.

Following me, Cherri undresses and says, "It's more where that came from."

Now, I am curious.

Chapter 18
JaNae

Things are going well. It looks like I'm headed in the right direction to start my career path. Being a business major is such broad a spectrum, and I hadn't pinpointed where I was going with it. The more research I did, the more I realized that event planning was what I want to do. It's all about relationships: relationships with vendors as well clients and that is right up my alley. My mother has so many connections throughout the city, and this of course works in my favor for future internships.

The semester is over, and the city is on fire. It is nice just being home and in my own bed. My favorite part of coming home is that I am hella spoiled, and my momma cooks all of my favorite foods. Being an only child, I have it like that. My Aunt Veronica needs a receptionist at her investment firm, so I have a summer job lined up.

The hours are great, 9 to 5 Monday through Thursday, and the ability to pick her brain at a more intimate level on investing is a win-win. I saw my mom struggle to get on her feet sometimes when I was younger, and I learned from her mistakes. You have to prepare for your future. If you fail to prepare, you're prepared to fail. So, this summer job will turn into so much more.

"Nae, how about we go on a vacation? I booked us a cruise. You've been doing so well in school, I want to do something special for you," my mom says smiling.

"Seriously Ma? Thank you so much. My girls are gonna flip. "

"I already know. I put down the deposits for all four of us. They just need to pay the rest," my mom tells me.

"Ahh, I can't believe you did that! Girl give me some sugar," I say planting kisses all over her face. I notice she is a little warm.

"Nae quit before you mess up my make up, gal. You need to be giving me kisses like this all the time," she scolds.

"You know I looove you mama, seriously. You feeling okay? You seem a bit warm.

"Momma is just fine. You know what, I slept under that fan last night. I'll be okay. I'll give you the American Express so you can go shopping. I know you're going to love that."

"This day just keeps getting better and better. I'm going to call Bri and Denise and tell them the good news. Where are we going Ma?"

"I'm taking y'alls little non-virgin asses to the Virgin Islands," she says, cracking up.

"Ma, you know you crazy!"

"You have to live life to the fullest every day. It's time for us to have some fun. Now go call those sidekicks of yours and yes, I know I'm awesome."

Wow, my mama has really outdone herself! I had no idea she was planning a trip, and this is exactly what I need. From the pictures I've seen, the Virgin Islands is a beautiful place to visit and even get married. I would love to plan an event there just because of the culture alone. Maybe in the future. Let's see what happens with James.

My family and I planned a dinner for mom's birthday, which is a few days before we leave for our trip. A few things about my mom Janice is that she loves being around people and she loves seafood. About 25-30 of our closest friends and relatives are attending the surprise dinner. Ms. Thing is turning 55, so we're celebrating by having everyone wear white. Her favorite color is yellow, so I got her a new yellow dress and a white Kate Spade purse. I also got her a special locket with a picture of the both of us enclosed inside.

I love this lady with all of my heart, and when I become a successful business tycoon she will want for nothing. I would love for her to relax and enjoy the life the Lord gave her. Her little guy friend, Mr. Larry, was happy to see her happy. Mr. Larry has an IT firm and has been waiting to settle down and retire with momma. They are too cute together. He has been in the picture for the last eight years and to him that lady can do no wrong. He never oversteps or tries to be my dad, but he loves me and has always supported me alongside my mom. I respect and love him for making my mom happy.

I sit back and watch my momma. She seems so grateful and "in the moment." I love sitting back just watching her in her element. It's a blessing to have such an amazing role model in my life. She is always the life of the party, and everyone that comes in contact with her has no choice but to love her. Momma is a kindhearted and giving person and didn't take any shortcuts. She doesn't spare feelings, but that's the realness in her. You might not like the way she says something, but you have to respect it and she will never steer you wrong.

"Can I have everyone's attention, if you don't mind?" Mr. Larry stands up and asks. "Jay you are my world, so please say you'll make me the happiest man alive by being my wife!" he asks as he pulls out a beautiful engagement ring.

My jaw hits the damn floor. I had no idea he had a surprise within the surprise party. He asked her years ago, but she said she liked the way things were between them and she loved her independence. Lord, I hope she doesn't embarrass this man.

"Baby, I would love to marry you," she says, kissing him on the lips. Partygoers are in awe, and this moment is proof that it is never too late for love. Love has no age or limit. Momma puts that fat rock on her finger and looks like she is loving life. After the commotion dies down, she excuses herself and heads to the lady's room, so I pass out the rest of the cake before I go to privately congratulate her. I walk into the lady's room to see that my mother is very upset.

"What's wrong Ma? You okay? Is the party too much or something?" I ask, grabbing tissues to dab her eyes so she won't ruin her makeup.

"No baby, nothing like that. Momma is just having a moment that's all. I'm just fine. Don't mind me."

"You sure Ma? I hope nobody upset you. Was the proposal too much? That was *all* Mr. Larry on that solo mission. I had no idea."

"No sweetheart. I promise you are good. Let's get

back out to the party. Give me a minute. I will be right out," she tells me.

It's her birthday, so reluctantly I let her be and stop asking questions. I fix her make up so that she looks flawless once again, but this conversation isn't over by any means. Even though she tried to brush me off, the look in her eyes said much more and she knows I know something isn't right. After a few moments, she returns to the birthday gathering as if nothing was bothering her at all, and she makes it known that we are now officially in countdown mode as paradise awaits us.

The time has finally come to get out on the open seas. The luxury cruise liner has a long list of amenities including casinos, a mall, pools, water slides, clubs, three gyms, child care, restaurants, an ice bar, and a 4D cinema. Let's not forget to mention the acts and concerts that were scheduled during our 4-day trip. I can't wait to see some of the performance. They have comedians, singers, magicians, and even a burlesque show. I instantly start a soulful rendition of "Under the Sea" from *The Little Mermaid* to myself. Once we check in and put our bags down, Momma decides to go to the casino while we explore the ship to see what we can get ourselves into. This is my mom's third cruise, so she chuckles at our excitement.

"I will meet up with you girls at 7 in the main dining lounge for dinner. That will give you time to look around. Listen ladies, if you can't get yourselves out of it, don't get yourselves into it," she warns while giving us the eye. That lets me know she means business.

"Alright Momma. You know we're good girls for the most part. See you at dinner," I say, giving her multiple kisses on her cheek.

"See you later Ms. Jay," Bri says while waving good-bye and Denise, always the character says, "Ms. Jay don't be catching no young men on this cruise girl," and we all laugh.

It's time to explore. New adventures await us; three baddies walking around in bikini tops and shorts and the men on this boat look finger licking good! All eyes are on us while we sashay around the boat getting to know our surroundings. We'd already planned our days with massages, shopping, and pool parties. We have all inclusive wristbands that guarantee us that anything we want to eat or drink is at our disposal, and our glasses will remain full during the entire trip. We are having a damn good time.

Basking in the glow of the sun adds a nice bronze glow to our skin and sharing this time with my mom and my girls is priceless. *This* is how you live. I can't believe my mom has been holding out one me. Hey, that's what happens when you work hard, you play harder. We couldn't have asked for more out of a vacation. We have done so much in these past few days while making beautiful memories. We have been partying by the pool, snorkeling, and we even went horseback riding on the beach during one of our excursions. When we dock in Galveston tomorrow, I'll be able to post all of my pics. We have taken what seems like thousands of them. It's hard getting back to the real world when you have had a piece of paradise. Can vacationing become a profession? Hell, only in my dreams I suppose. All I know is The Virgin Islands don't owe us a thing!

When nightfall approaches, we head to the room to get ready for dinner and since every meal has been a fashion show, who am I to deny them all this sexy on our last night? Denise is our designated makeup artist, so she has put in an extra effort to make sure our makeup matches our ensembles for the evening. I'm a glitter queen so my smoked-out cat eye has gold glitter to accent my yellow, floor- length sundress with a slit up to the middle of my thick thigh. My six-inch stilettos keep men's mouths on the floor every time they look at my calves. "Give the people what they want," is what I always say.

Bri is killing it with a white two-piece, a form fitting mid-drift top, and knee length pencil skirt showing off her toned six pack. Multi-crystal strappy Steve Madden pumps takes her outfit to another level. Not much for makeup, she just rocks mascara, black liner, and a nude lip.

Denise will never let anyone outshine her, so she wears a short, black bodycon dress with sheer material along both sides complimented by red high heeled sandals. She chose them to match her red matt lips. Needless to say, baby girl is not concerned with panty lines. My crew is looking like a bag of money, if I do say so myself.

Once we reach the table to join my mom, the waiter takes our drink orders, not able to keep his eyes above our breasts while stumbling over his words. Poor guy. Denise gives him a wink, and he turns beet red.

"I knew the moment y'all came into the door because heads immediately turned in your direction. One woman smacked her husband for staring so hard," my mom manages to say between her laughter. We all join in with her.

"Ms. Jay, God didn't give us all of this to hide it," Denise adds.

"I can't take the three of y'all nowhere!" momma says, shaking her head at us.

To finish off our last dinner on the ship, we are served a three-course meal fit for a Queen, and we enjoy every morsel. We are stuffed. You can't beat good food and good company.

"We need to go dance all of this food off at one of the night life spots. After this food settles first. Whew!" Bri rubs her tummy, which has started to protrude due to the generous portion she ate. It kind of surprises us because her stomach is usually flat.

"Baby, I'm not feeling the best so I'm going back to the room. I'm going to call it a night," my mother says.

"Let's go. You know I'll take care of you," I say.

"No, no . . . I'll be okay, just let me just go lay down for a spell. You girls enjoy your night. Don't forget that if you need anything just charge it to the room. You know not to lose your everlasting minds, but this trip was for you girls to have fun. I'll see you in the morning."

"Are you sure Ma? It's no problem. I can come with you," I assure her.

"I'm just probably a little sea sick. I'll see you in the morning," she says, kissing me on the forehead.

I'm sure if she needs me she will let me know. I walk her to her room anyway, just to make sure she is comfortable.

The girls and I move this party to the hip hop club called Nite Life, and men are buying us drinks left and right so we were feeling good.

"I've got something to tell y'all, and I can't hold it in anymore," Denise says. Bri and I look concerned and we're ready to see what the problem is.

"I've been seeing somebody. I didn't want to say anything until I knew it was worth telling you, especially after all of the bullshit with Al."

"WHAAAT," we say in unison.

"We need the who, what, when, and where so come off the details ma'am!" I quiz. We live for juicy gossip.

"Y'all can't trip or be all judgmental and shit…fuck it, it's Cherri," she continues as she braces herself for our responses.

"Bitch you lying!" Bri covers her mouth in shock.

"Never saw that one coming. Hey no judgment here. I love you for you. Long as you not trying to get in my pants we cool! Bwaaaaaaaaa!" I say as we all erupt in laughter.

Denise begins to tell the story of her and Cherrie. She told us about what happened when we left her apartment, when her and Cherri hooked up. She tells us Cherri opened her mind to something new that she wants to explore. We are not the type of friends to turn or backs on each other. We just want to see each other happy so, of course, Bri and I offer her our full support.

Hours are rolling by like minutes and we have been consuming alcohol like it is water all night. Now this Patron has me feeling some kind of way, and that way is horny. Technically, I am not spoken for, so I am within my right to have sex with whomever I please and Mr. Right Now is a very handsome gentleman by the name of Terrell Sams from Florida A&M. I am ready to see what he is working with. Blame it on the alcohol, like Jamie Foxx says. You only live once, right? The girls got the room number where I was headed, for safety reasons, then I was out. Baby, I am on vacation, so I am doing me.

But less than 30 minutes later, I am heated from disappointment when leaving Terrell's room. The walk over there and make out session was longer than the amount of time he actually stayed in the pussy. He was working with a nice sized piece, but couldn't do a damn thing with it. Hitting it extremely fast and hard didn't do a thing for me. That boy's stroke game was weak, and it wasn't sexy at all. I can't believe he had sweat dripping down his damn face like he was putting in work. Um no sir! Before I could get anything out of it, the shit was over, and he collapsed beside me. The dick was trash. I mean, really dude.

Was I getting punked? Stella didn't get her groove back tonight. Why does TV make vacation sex look so romantic? Everything happened so fast with the tequila guiding me, that I regretfully misplaced my mind and forgot about a condom. First thing on my list in the morning is to head to the on-board pharmacy for a Plan B pill. I could slap myself right now. Ughhh.

This vacation is officially over and I need to go check on my momma. As I walk down the hallway approaching her room, I hear a bunch of commotion. My God! They are wheeling her out on a stretcher!

"Ma, what's going on?!" I scream. Her eyes are closed, and an oxygen mask is covering her nose and mouth. At this point everything begins moving in slow motion. When we reach the medical services area on the boat, the doctor starts spitting off questions I can't answer. Bri and Denise are holding my hands as we pray for my mother.

Bri found my mom's insurance card so medical services can call her family doctor to get more information. An ambulance will be waiting on us in an hour and a half when we get to the port. The girls go to get our belongings together so we will be ready to disembark as soon as possible. We change clothes and throw on sweats and tennis shoes, not worried about what we look like. While rushing down the hallway back towards where they are holding my mother, I run into Terrell.

"JaNae what's going on? When I woke up you were gone," he says.

"My mother is ill, and we have to get out of here," I say walking past him. I don't owe him any explanation, and I can't think straight. Once I make it back to my mom, I call Mr. Larry and our family doctor to update them with what is going on with my mother. They assure me that they will be at the hospital when we get there. Thank God Dr. Poland has privilege in multiple hospitals and is willing to meet us at the University of Texas Medical Center in Galveston. I'm scared out of my mind!

At the hospital, Dr. Poland finally enters the room with a look of concern as he reads my mother's chart.

"JaNae, may I speak with you alone please?" he asks. Mr. Larry, Bri, and Denise start to get up to leave.

"This is family. Whatever you have to say, you can say it in front of them," I say, looking at my girls and Mr. Larry.

"I don't know why your mother was out in the ocean with her health depleting the way it is. The cancer has now spread to her lymph nodes, and she's in a coma."

"Cancer? What are you talking about? Mr. Larry did

you know anything about this?" I cry as I stumble backwards.

"Lord knows, I didn't know. My God, Jay didn't tell me anything. Why baby, why didn't you tell me? We were planning our wedding!" He begins to cry as well.

"JaNae, your mother was diagnosed with Stage 3 Breast Cancer two years ago. After her first round of chemo, she refused any other treatment. She has been my patient for over 15 years. I begged her to seek treatment of some type, and to talk to her support system."

"So, what do we do at this point? What do we need to do to fight this? Please tell me there is something we can do?" I'm in disbelief. None of this is making sense to me.

"The cancer has spread throughout her body at this point, so we can only make her comfortable. I'm so sorry. I'm going to suggest that she gets a transfer to a hospice facility."

"We were just on a cruise, and she was fine. Now she's headed to hospice. Why didn't she tell us? Momma why? She didn't have to go through this alone. What am I going to do without my momma?!" I scream. That unfortunate reality is what stares at me in the mirror. We all hold each other and cry throughout the night.

When her vitals are stable enough, momma is transported to a hospice facility in Houston. I want her to be home so our family and friends can visit her. Momma never regains consciousness from the coma, and in less than 2 weeks' time, Janice Elizabeth Woods is gone, surrounded by friends and love ones. It feels like a blink of an eye. Nothing could ever prepare me for this, but I know He would not put more on me than I can bare.

I thank God that my mom took care of her business. So many in the black community leave this earth and leave their families in a strain to pick up the pieces after such a loss. I had no idea she had three polices where I was the beneficiary, and she made sure to take care of Mr. Larry too. I would trade it all to get her back. I know she didn't tell me because she didn't want me to drop out of school to care for her.

I go into business mode and take care of the intimate details of the service. Her favorite flowers, limos for family members, and a breathtaking picture of her for the memorial. As hard as it is, the homegoing service is very well put together. I think I'm fine, and that I've made my piece with her leaving before this day. But when that casket is closed, never to be opened again, it actually registers to me that my mother is gone for good. This is not a bad dream. I totally lose it, screaming to the point that my uncles have to carry me out of the funeral home.

After the funeral, I'm drained. I don't want to be around anyone. James, bless his heart, has tried to be there for me, but I am genuinely inconsolable. I push him away, which is easy since we just started getting to know each other not too long ago. I want to sleep away the pain. Wine got me through the last few days because I didn't want to feel anything. Bri and Denise aren't going to let that last forever, and I will forever love them for not letting me slip into an abyss. They reminded me that my mother was a strong woman who wouldn't want me to be this way. My girls keep assuring me that, no matter what, they are not leaving my side and even though feel so alone, I will always have them.

Epilogue
Five Years Later
JaNae

Double checking everything from top to bottom, this wedding is together. My staff knows my expectations and that means I expect perfection. Being the Maid of Honor, I cannot dedicate the proper time needed to plan the entire event. I trust my staff completely, but this is the most important wedding we have done to date. How could it not be? My best friend Brianna and the love of her life, Chase, are tying the knot. I am beyond excited for her and slightly jealous because I want my Boaz. But overall, I am truly happy for my friend.

The bridal suite is stacked with champagne and strawberries as well as light hor d'oeuvres so that the ladies are not getting beautiful on an empty stomach. It's three hours until the show starts. Surprisingly, Bri is just as calm as could be. She was laughing and singing with the cutest flower girl I had ever seen.

"Hi mommy! I'm helping God Ma Bri get ready to

marry Uncle Chase."

"That's a good girl Angel," I tell her.

Angel is literally my heartbeat. After my mother passed away from breast cancer five years ago, I felt lost. I memorized the letter she left behind:

> *Finding out that my cancer was at Stage 3 was devastating. My first thought was, "I'm going to fight this thing and win." But, that chemo kicked my ass every-which way from Sunday and I refused to pump anymore of that poison into my body. I didn't want people to feel sorry for me. This was one battle I would fight alone. JaNae and Larry, it hurt my soulnot to tell you my truth, but I didn't want either of you to stop your lives to take care of me. I want you to remember me for the good times, not tears of pain. I know money does not make up for all of the time I will miss out on, but I don't want you, or my future grandbabies, to want for anything. To all that I cherished so dear, a piece of me resides in your heart always. I apologize to any that are hurt at my expense. My journey is my own, and I regret nothing about it.*
>
> *Sincerely and lovingly yours,*
> *Janice Woods "Jay"*

Finding out that I was pregnant was a beautiful tragedy that snapped me back to reality. Unfortunately, it was not the family I always imagined because she was not conceived between a husband and wife or two people in love. I regretted getting pregnant from that one night stand, but I do not regret the result. With everything that happened with my mom, I forgot to get the

Plan B pill, and now I am glad I did. I prayed for a healthy birth and for my child to be healthy, smart, beautiful and for her to look like me. This little girl was my spitting image, just add a Marilyn Monroe mole on her lip and piercing grey eyes. Momma would have spoiled my baby rotten; her first grand baby.

My right hand in planning this wedding was my other best friend, Denise. She threw a bachelorette party that should be banned in some states. We had male and female strippers, a toy presentation, and a class on giving head. As soon as I get a sex life again I will be trying some of those tricks to trap my man . . .

Connect with the Author

Website: www.dvinepen.com

Facebook: D'Vine Pen

Instagram: @dvinepen

Twitter: @dvinepen

Creative Control With Self-Publishing

Divine Legacy Publishing provides authors with the guid-ance necessary to take creative control of their work through self-publishing. We provide:

Let Divine Legacy Publishing help you master the business of self-publishing.

www.ingramcontent.com/pod-product-compliance
Lightning Source LLC
Chambersburg PA
CBHW071001120726
47910CB00004B/1339